For Marion and Duncan Mundell,
my cousins in Glasgow, Scotland,
with all my love

MOLLY

CHAPTER ONE

The Atlantic liner gave a great heave, shuddered, wallowed in the trough, and groaned its way up the next wave.

Molly Maguire clutched her little sister, Mary, closer to her on the stateroom bed as the great liner creaked and juddered its way through the storm, and thought miserably, *This is how cattle must feel. Here we are, two poor little American cows on our way to England to be mated.*

Mary whimpered with fright as the ship gave another monumental heave, and their ex-schoolteacher-companion, Miss Simms, let out a shriek and took an enormous pull at her bottle of gin.

Miss Simms looked with lackluster eyes at the beautiful Maguire sisters and reflected dully that she should never have accepted this post, no matter how much the money.

And as for Molly, she wished they were all back in the cosy comfort of her father's shop in Brooklyn, when things were safe and normal before that momentous evening a year ago when she and Mary had unwittingly founded the Maguire fortunes.

She closed her eyes tightly to shut out the motion of the ship and remembered how it had all begun. . . .

It had been a close, humid Brooklyn evening in Jane Street, a narrow alley running off Fulton Street in downtown Brooklyn. The gas lamps had been lit, the other, bigger stores—Namm's, Frederick Loeser's, Waldorf Shoes—had all put up their shutters long ago. But the Maguire's General Store stayed open, sometimes around the clock, in order to lure stray customers to their doors. They sold everything and anything from hairpins to coffee beans. Mr. Joseph Maguire and his wife, Nadia, had retired to bed leaving their daughters, Molly and Mary, to cope with any late-night shoppers.

The large flyblown mirror over the unused

fireplace, advertising Bigg's Tobacco in curly glass letters, reflected their tired faces; a beautiful combination of vivid blue eyes and black curly hair from their Irish father and the high Slav cheekbones of their Polish mother. The girls often took turns sleeping on a mattress under the counter. If anyone had told them that their life was hard, they would have been very surprised indeed. Both were dutiful, lively, and merry. They passed the long night hours weaving romantic fantasies. The shop bell would clang and who should be standing on the threshold but the Prince of Ruritania himself. He would fall in love with one of them, of course. Molly said it would be Mary and Mary swore loyally it would be Molly.

But usually it was only one of the local lads with his sheepish smile and thick boots, giggling and asking for "two ounces of baccy."

The neighbors were apt to censure the Maguire parents for exposing their daughters to the dangers of nighttime Brooklyn. But Molly kept a shotgun under the counter, which her father had taught her to use, and Officer Brady made as many calls as he could to stand and drink coffee in the warmth of the little shop and admire the famous beauty of the girls.

On the fateful evening that was to change their lives, Molly had just celebrated her seventeenth birthday. Mary was nearly sixteen. The hour was eleven in the evening and the shop no longer shook with the rumble of the trains on the King's County Elevated Railroad that ran above Fulton Street.

Molly was not feeling her usual happy-go-lucky self. Jimmy Heimlich, whose father owned the greengrocers two doors away, had asked her to walk out with him, but she had refused. And her mother had been very angry. Jimmy was a well-set-up young man and Mrs. Maguire had looked forward to a merging of the two businesses. Jimmy's father was failing, everyone knew that. It was only a matter of time. But her infuriating daughter had said no and had refused to give a reason.

Molly could not really work out in her mind *why* she had refused Jimmy. At last she had said slowly that it was because she was not in love with Jimmy, and her angry mother had confiscated her small store of romances, saying she could not have her books back until she came to her senses.

The theater crowd from Colonel William F. Simm's Park Theater had cheered the Spooner Stock Company to the last curtain call and had gone home without any of them calling in at the Maguires' store. It looked as if it were going to be a quiet night.

Mary was asleep under the counter because she had school in the morning. Molly, who

12

had finished school, had elected to stay awake.

But her eyes felt heavy and she leaned her elbows on the counter, enduring the familiar feeling of fatigue and sore feet. Her eyelids drooped lower and lower and the temptation to crawl under the counter beside Mary was nearly irresistible.

The sudden clanging of the doorbell brought her eyes open with a jerk, and then she blinked. For surely the lady standing on the threshold must have come from one of her dreams.

Despite the close humidity of the night, she was dressed from head to foot in white ermine. She had a thin, white, autocratic face with weak, pale eyes. On her scarlet hair was perched a sequined cap ornamented with long black cock's feathers that hung down to her shoulder. She raised a hand to her forehead and her furred cuff fell back to reveal a heavy diamond bracelet circling a wrist so fragile and thin that you would have thought it would have snapped under the weight of the jewels.

Behind her stood a tall elderly gentleman with a white mustache and a florid face. Little beads of moisture clung to his tall silk hat and to the fur collar of his coat.

And behind the couple a huge Lozier automobile crouched beside the curb, with a uniformed chauffeur standing at attention.

It must be a dream!

13

But the lady was moving forward languidly to the counter. She opened her thin, painted mouth and said, "Hev youse got anything for dis cough? It's a-makin' me sick to my stummick, ain't it, Joey?"

"Yaas," said the elderly gentleman vaguely, and then, "What's thet?"

"Thet" was Mary's round eyes peering over the counter. Mary got to her feet and smoothed out the creases on her starched pinafore and both Maguire sisters stared at their customers in awe.

"Come along, gels," said the gentleman called Joey. "Meh Dolores hes got the cough something awful, she has."

And in answer Dolores let out a series of stentorian barks. "Theh you ah!" said Joey triumphantly. The gentleman appeared to be English, to judge from the strangulated accents coming from him. But his fair lady had undoubtedly sprung from Brooklyn soil. Molly looked feverishly around the shop. No cough medicine.

She stood irresolute. She did not want to send these grand customers away empty-handed. Then Molly remembered her grandmother's old receipt book in the back shop. Surely there would be something in that.

"We have just the thing, if you will wait a few minutes," said Molly, nipping deftly around the counter and placing a chair for Dolores next to the shelves of canned goods. And hustling the wide-eyed Mary in front of her, she bustled into the back shop.

"What are you *doing*?" demanded Mary. "We ain't got no cough syrup."

"Haven't got any," corrected Molly automatically. "But there's bound to be something in Gran's book. Here it is! Now, let me see—*cough, cough, cough*—ah, got it! Find an empty bottle, Mary, and draw a label—you're good at that—and call it . . . oh, something fancy."

While Mary seized her ever ready paints and paper, Molly got to work. In a small bowl she mixed fennel, cinnamon, anise, and lemon and added two spoonfuls of honey. It needed more. It needed something to bring these fabulous people back to the Maguire store. Alcohol! That was it! Coming as she did from a Polish-Irish background, Molly was convinced that adults were fueled solely by alcohol. Her mother's bottle of 140 proof Polish vodka stood over by the sink. She added a great slug to the mixture and turned to see how Mary was getting on.

Mary had cut one of her small drawings out of her pad. It showed a rather evil-looking leprechaun sitting on a rock, leering up at several fairies who were dancing through a rainbow overhead. Mary had quickly added the words MAGUIRES' LEPRECHAUN DEW in bold black gothic lettering.

"Oh, that's very good. But it's awful, too," laughed Molly. "They'll know we're taking the Mickey."

"Come along, gels," trumpeted the voice of Joey. "Meh Dolores is waiting."

"It'll have to do," hissed Molly, pasting the label on the bottle. "Here goes!"

"This is our own recipe," said Molly sweetly, handing Dolores the bottle. Dolores looked suspiciously at the leprechaun who seemed to look suspiciously back, but Joey was already pulling out a purse and demanding the price. Molly thought quickly. She did not want to charge too little. She did not want to charge too much. She took a deep breath. "Fifty cents, please," she said. "It's a very old recipe and we don't give it to many customers."

"It had better work or youse'll hear from me," said Dolores nastily. Joey was looking at the Maguire sisters in a way Molly did not like.

When the door had crashed shut behind the customers, Molly and Mary remained standing primly behind the counter until they could hear the car no longer. Then they both burst out into peals of laughter, hanging on to each other. "Leprechaun Dew, indeed," howled Mary. Then she sobered. "But why are you always after me to talk proper, Molly? She *don't*. I mean she talked like a regular Brooklyner."

Molly hesitated. And then, lowering her voice, she said, "I think Dolores was that man's *mistress*."

"Oooohl" screamed Mary in gleeful dismay. Then her face fell. "It's a pity if she is. Thought she was one of them East Siders who'd take a fancy to us and introduce us to society, where we would meet a prince."

Molly gave her an affectionate hug. "Let's forget about the whole thing. Wouldn't Ma be mad if she knew what we'd done!"

Perhaps Mrs. Maguire would never have heard of their visitors had they been sold something other than cough medicine. Dolores moved on the fringes of the best circles, where she was only barely tolerated because of her protector's great wealth. No lady was going to listen to Miss Dolores's views on anything. Anything, that is, but the common cold, that most democratic of minor illnesses.

The stunned Maguire parents found themselves being besieged during the following week for Maguires' Leprechaun Dew. The secret was out and the custom was in as Molly mixed and filled and Mary drew and painted and the limousines and carriages blocked the narrow lane outside.

By the following week the Maguires were closing up shop very early indeed so that they could cope with the flood of orders. Neither parents had any proper business sense and the whole thing might have fizzled out for lack of supplies, but Fate decided to take a further hand in the presence of Mr. Bernard Abrahams who ran the tailoring shop next door.

Mr. Abrahams was in his thirties and had recently and gloomily inherited the business from his father and was reputed to make the worst suits in the whole of Brooklyn. But Bernie had also recently discovered a talent for turning money into more money by gambling shrewdly on Wall Street. He elected himself advisor to the bewildered Maguires. With his beaky nose and brightly colored waistcoats, he darted around the Maguires' small living room above the shop like some strange bird of paradise. Soon a small factory in Red Hook was turning out the precious bottles of cough mixture, and the huge bull-like figure of Mr. Maguire twisted and turned to follow Bernie's mad gyrations and his large cauliflower ears strained to take in a flood of talk about stocks and shares and distributors and international markets.

Now that the factory was in operation, Molly and Mary felt somewhat at a loss. The work and bustle had gone now that bottles of Maguires' Leprechaun Dew were now appearing in all the major pharmacies.

One evening after she had put up the heavy wooden shutters, Molly climbed the stairs to their small dark living room to find Bernie, as usual, holding the floor. Her mother had been darning a sock but it lay limply in her hand as she turned her large, dazed white face to Bernie's small animated one. "Millionaires!" she was saying faintly.

"Ain't it the truth," said Bernie, hooking his thumbs in his waistcoat and then peering down to admire the gleaming white of his new spats. "So you've gotta move in with the nobs, now . . . see. Can't go on living in a rat hole like this."

Mrs. Nadia Maguire looked dazedly around the dark living room. "But what will we do? What will happen to the girls?"

"They'll become ladies, that's what," said Bernie. "As for you, Ma, don't you want to travel? See the Riviera and places like that? I'll find a companion for the girls. One of their schoolteachers'll do the trick."

And that, reflected Molly, had been the beginning of the end. They had moved to a great dark brownstone in Brooklyn Heights with Miss Simms, their former English teacher, as companion while their parents went off on a world tour.

19

Miss Simms was a brisk, ferrety woman who hid a penchant for gin under an energetic exterior. Her way of introducing the girls to Brooklyn Heights society was to inform them that their neighbors were "common" and to take them for long, dreary walks on the Promenade. They still wore their plaid school dresses and white starched aprons and had their uncomfortable boots bought for them for two dollars and fifty cents a pair at the Waldorf Shoe Company in Fulton Street. They could do little else about it for Miss Simms held the purse strings. Bernie would occasionally relieve the monotony of their existence by taking them to Dreamland, the great pleasure park at Surf Avenue and West Eighth Street, where they could do their own world tour through four simulated corners of the globe. But mostly he was absorbed in his business affairs.

Then at last the Maguire parents returned, much changed. Mrs. Maguire seemed to think it fashionable to appear chronically ill. Her fat figure had dwindled to angular lines and she perpetually held a long, trailing handkerchief in one hand and a bottle of smelling salts in the other. Pa Maguire had adopted what he fondly believed to be an English accent and rivaled Bernie in the brightness of his waistcoats and the whiteness of his spats. But the homecoming welcomes were hardly over when the last blow fell. The Maguire parents had arranged for Molly and Mary to travel to England.

They were to stay with a certain Lady Fanny Holden at a fashionable English resort called Hadsea. There they would be polished and molded and prepared for a London Season. They would both marry lords and live happily ever after.

Mary began to cry. Everything had been taken away. Her school, the cosy shop, the work, their home, and now their parents. Molly stood protectively over her, prepared to do battle. But the arrival of Bernie knocked the wind out of her sails. For Bernie, noisy, garrulous Bernie, whom she had looked upon as an uncle, was equally enraged. He, Bernie, had planned to marry Molly. Caught between Scylla and Charybdis, Molly found she had nothing to say.

She would look on the bright side of things. Perhaps when they sailed to England there would be other young people on board the liner. There might even be a prince, she told Mary.

So two white-faced and sad American misses set sail on the great liner *Titania*. And right into one of the worst of the Atlantic storms.

CHAPTER TWO

The beaten and battered *Titania* crept up the oily estuary waters of Southampton as one by one the shaking passengers began to emerge on deck, most of them for the first time. They walked up and down, talking in shocked whispers and staring in awe at the battered superstructure of the ship. The ship's doctor bustled from cabin to cabin with his black bag, ministering to those who had not yet recovered from the horrendous journey.

The Maguire sisters huddled together for comfort beside the rail and stared in dismay at what they could make out of their new homeland. A steady drizzle was falling from a dark-gray sky. The clouds were so low that they lay in great sodden masses along the low hills of the Southampton estuary. It all looked bleak and unfriendly and *foreign*.

Both were reflecting dismally on what Miss Simms had told them in a fit of drunken venom. "Think you're going to marry lords?" the ex-schoolteacher had hiccuped. "Why, they'll laugh in your faces."

"B-but Lady Fanny—" Molly had stuttered.

"Her!" sneered Miss Simms. "She'd groom a pair of Hottentots for the London Season. She's being *paid* to do it. You're nobody special."

It was then that Molly had felt a cold rage taking possession of her.

"You, Miss Simms," she said with an edge to her voice that Mary had never heard her use before, "are also being paid to be a *companion* and not a drunken, venomous mentor. I am dismissing you."

"You always were a fresh kid," retorted Miss Simms indifferently. "Cheese it. You ain't firing nobody. Your pa hired me and your pa fires me. So there."

She had then turned back to her ever constant companion, her bottle of gin, leaving Molly to stare at her with baffled fury.

Now as they stood at the rail, Mary said suddenly, "Perhaps if we behave very badly, Lady Fanny will send us home."

Molly straightened her spine and stared out at the dark shores of England. "No we won't, Mary. We're American. We're democratic. We'll do our best, and if they don't like it, they can send us home." A sudden vision of the cosy shop in Jane Street, with its cluttered sacks and cans of goods, its smell of spices and coffee and candy, sprang into her mind; a little world shielded from the dark by the warm flare of the gaslight. And then she realized that her home was gone and her parents—two posturing strangers she did not recognize. Two salt tears rolled down her cheeks, adding their moisture to that of the now steadily falling rain.

The bustle of departure from the ship went by like a rain-soaked dream. The press swarmed over the *Titania*, taking photographs of the storm damage and lightening the dark day with their magnesium flashes. Ignoring a very white-faced Miss Simms, the Maguire sisters walked arm in arm to the barrier and noticed, still as if in a dream, that a smartly dressed footman was holding up a placard bearing their names.

In no time at all, they were cosily tucked up in rugs in a large traveling carriage and bowling away from the bustle of the port, with the coachman gaily cracking his whip and two enormous footmen perched up behind.

Molly was glad to see that Miss Simms was

beginning to look cowed. The Maguire sisters had been treated with every deference and Miss Simms with practically none at all. In fact, one of the footmen had taken a contemptuous sniff of the strong aroma of gin that surrounded the companion, had given Miss Simms one scandalized look, and then retreated to his post. Miss Simms began to chew peppermint pastilles as hard as she could and kept muttering that she wished she had not come.

Their journey was broken at a large inn and it was there that Molly first became aware of how strange they must look.

Both girls were dressed in their green-and-white plaid school dresses covered with their best starched aprons. All their clothes were to be bought for them in England so Mrs. Maguire had thoughtlessly provided nothing new for the journey. Molly had grown since leaving school and she realized, to her embarrassment, that she was showing an unseemly expanse of ankle. The dining room of the inn seemed to her unsophisticated eyes to be extremely richly furnished, with its deep turkey-red carpet and its small, glittering chandeliers.

Every time she said something to Mary, everyone in the dining room would stop eating. They did not stare, they were too polite for that. They simply sat and listened and then leaned their heads together and whispered.

Molly had cut up her roast beef and vegetables and was eating it all with her fork. But this, she realized, was completely the wrong thing to do. It seemed one must use *both* knife and fork at the same time and hold them rather like pencils. It was all very strange.

All too soon they were back on the road, bowling between high hedgerows that filled the carriage with green gloom, up little rises past tiny farms—like farms in a children's storybook.

Molly's head was beginning to droop. The lunch had been heavy and she was feeling sleepy.

"Hadsea!" called the coachman, and she straightened up. Mary and Miss Simms had both fallen asleep, the latter snoring with her mouth open and her once jaunty straw hat askew. Molly let down the carriage window and looked out. The carriage was winding down a steep road. On the right, the sea seemed to stretch to infinity, and as they turned another bend the heavy clouds parted and a broad, sparkling ray of sunshine lit up the little town nestling in the curve of the bay.

The clouds parted more and more as the carriage wound down the hill. Colors sprang magically out of the dark landscape. Great clumps of sea pinks clung to outcrops in the springy turf, harebells quivered in a light breeze, a whole field of buttercups blazed out to welcome the return of summer, and brightly painted fishing boats bobbed and danced at anchor on a sea of pure aquamarine. And a long curve of golden sand bordered with little creamy waves stretched around the length of the bay.

The Maguire sisters and summer had arrived at Hadsea.

Lady Fanny Holden gave a final authoritative twitch to a vase full of roses and, having decided that they had been properly disciplined, turned to her husband, Lord Toby, as the next thing that needed to be put in order.

"Now, Toby," she barked, "it's no use standing there shuffling and muttering in that irritating way that it's all a bore. The gels will be here shortly and you must change. You are *not* an example of an English gentleman of the aristocracy in that filthy old tweed jacket. I shall never forget the humiliation the day I gave it to the church sale and found that you had bought it back."

Lady Fanny was an energetic woman in her fifties, with thick white skin, pale-blue eyes, and well-ordered salt-and-pepper hair. She was inclined to be plump but kept the unseemly bulges rigorously at bay in the confines of a long Empire corset.

Her husband had a hunted air. He was tall and thin with thick fair hair, a fair mustache that he kept fingering nervously, and rather bulging weak eyes. He was at that moment dressed in the offending jacket, an old pair of knickerbockers, worsted socks, and elderly brogues cracked and trodden into comfort. Sometimes it seemed to him that his whole married life had been a desperate search for ease and comfort, constantly stymied by the rigorous discipline of his wife.

For one whole beautiful summer last year he had enjoyed the peace of Hadsea while his wife chafed at the inactivity. He had pottered in the garden, stared at the sea, gone for long walks with his silent dogs, and occasionally dropped into the Prince of Wales down by the pier for a pint. Now all that had fled. His wife had insisted that they needed more money. Hadsea had become fashionable. Already other titles—the sort of bores one tried to avoid at the club—were all around, alive and well, doing Larsen exercises on the beach and generally mucking up the scenery.

Any money for the tutoring of the Maguire sisters seemed to have been used up already on a too-large army of supercilious servants who kept popping out of the shrubbery like damned jack-in-the-boxes to light his bloody cigar when he least bloody wanted it lit! His beloved garden was now the property of two crusty, gnarled Scottish gnomes with their numerous undergardeners who had a positive mania for making straight lines and bordering them with the shells from last night's dinner. It was downright upsetting to see the remains of one's *moules rémoulade* keeping a bed of petunias at bay.

Driven from the sitting room by the noise of carriage wheels outside and the impatient cluckings of his wife, he muttered and pottered his way upstairs.

Lady Fanny adjusted her enormous white lace hat to precisely the right angle—one inch more to the left would be rakish and one more to the right would be common—and turned with a smile of welcome on her face.

The Maguire sisters stood in the doorway, holding hands and looking at her "as if I had come out of the Ark" as she often said afterward.

Lady Fanny's opening words were typical. "Oh, dear, dear, *dear*. Those clothes. Horrid. What can your mama have been thinking of? And what's that?"

"Miss Simms. Our . . . er . . . companion," said Molly weakly.

"Then take it away. It won't do," said Lady Fanny, waving her gloved hand.

Miss Simms pushed past the sisters into the room. "Are you talking about me?"

"And you poor girls must be so exhausted after your journey," said Lady Fanny, ignoring Miss Simms completely. She touched the bell. "Wembley," she said to a stern individual in a striped waistcoat, "send for Miss Betts—the dressmaker, you know—and despatch this back to America."

Molly looked around the sitting room, over the tapestried chairs with their curled gilt arms; at her reflection in the old greenish mirror over the fireplace; at the bowls of flowers; but there was no sign of a package for America. Then she realized that Lady Fanny had been referring to Miss Simms.

So did Miss Simms.

"You can't do this," yelled that unfortunate lady. "You're worse'n the Bowery gangs."

Lady Fanny deigned to notice Miss Simms. "What's your name, woman?"

"It's Euphemia Simms."

"Well, Simms, from the smell of you and from your manner, you'd be far better back on the other side of the Atlantic. Good God! I do believe the woman is going to argue. Take her away, Wembley."

"Very good, my lady," said the butler, easing the infuriated companion toward the door. "There is a boat from Southampton tomorrow morning."

Miss Simms let out a despairing squawk. "Say something, Molly," she shrilled. But Molly remembered the isolation of Brooklyn Heights and the insolence of the boat and turned away. So Miss Simms departed from the room and their lives, leaving behind a faint odor of gin and peppermints.

The girls stood awkwardly while Lady Fanny walked around them, tugging at a crease here and a fold there. Both girls were wearing depressing felt hats: the kind, called by English schoolchildren, "pudding basin." With one large white muscular hand, Lady Fanny twitched the offending headgear first from Molly's head and then Mary's. The springy, black, glossy curls came tumbling in a cascade down the girls' backs and Lady Fanny caught her breath. Why, the girls were beautiful! Molly had perhaps too much determination in her square chin, but Mary's little heart-shaped face was perfection itself.

Molly found her courage and her voice. "If you please," she said firmly, "we are both very tired and would like to wash and change."

"Of course, of course," said Lady Fanny briskly. Another touch of the bell and the efficient Wembley was sent to fetch the housekeeper, Mrs. Barkins. Mrs. Barkins led the girls up a wide sunny staircase to the bedrooms. The house was quite modern, late Victorian, Molly judged. It was, she had gathered, the Holdens' summer residence. Lady Fanny had described it to Mrs. Maguire as their "little summer cottage—very rustic." The little cottage boasted at least thirty bedrooms. It was a vast, sprawling mansion, built like a small castle with mock battlements and even a few fake arrow slits let into the walls.

But the architect had fortunately not carried his passion for medievalism as far as the windows, which were large and square, affording glimpses of a perfect English garden, complete with tennis courts, rolling lawns, English oaks, and a gazebo.

Mrs. Barkins pushed open a heavy mahogany door. "This will be your room, miss," she said to Molly. She then led the way through a bright rose-decorated room that opened onto a little sitting room, on the far side of which was a door that led to Mary's room.

Both girls turned dark red with embarrassment when they realized that their small stock of shabby clothes had been neatly hung away and their worn and darned undergarments placed in the drawers.

"Goodge will be your maid," said Mrs. Barkins, who was a stout, motherly woman with eyes as hard as pebbles and whose aprons and petticoats crackled with so much starch that she emitted a sharp series of noises like little pistol shots every time she moved. "Goodge is a local girl," Mrs. Barkins was saying. "I trust you will see that she does her work properly."

"That is surely your job," said Molly sweetly.

Mrs. Barkins looked at her in amazement. She had been looking forward to a mild spot of bullying. After all, Americans were heathens and didn't know what was what. But this young American had a steely glint in her eye and a firm set to her jaw. Mrs. Barkins reluctantly dropped a curtsy.

"I'll see to it, miss."

When the door had closed behind her, Molly found that her hands were trembling. What did one do with a maid? She had never ordered anyone around in all her young life.

But when Goodge appeared, a shy apple-faced girl not much older than Molly herself, and stood in the doorway with her eyes down, twisting her apron nervously in her hands, Molly recovered her courage.

"Now, Goodge," she said, "you will find that we are not used to having a lady's maid and you, I gather, are new to the work. I guess we'll manage somehow between us. Okay?"

"Oh, yes, miss," said the gratified Goodge,

34

saving up that deliciously foreign "Okay" for use in the kitchen.

"We have not yet got our new wardrobes," Molly went on, "so you'll just need to pick out the best we have."

She gave the maid a beautiful smile. Molly had a warm and charming smile that had already broken many hearts in Fulton Street, and the shy and timid Goodge was completely bowled over.

She, Goodge, would be the best lady's maid ever. She marched briskly over to the wardrobe and picked out Molly's Sunday dress, of drab brown taffeta, with a sure hand.

"This will be just the thing, miss," said Goodge. "My lady is with the dressmaker now and you are to have ever such lovely clothes." Goodge set to work.

Molly found to her surprise that it was a pleasant novelty to be waited on. To have deft little hands to fasten up all those awkward hooks and buttons and to gently brush one's tangled hair.

Mary was still very shy. "Come to my room when she does me," she whispered.

The next hour went by with bewildering speed as the exhausted girls were turned this way and that and pinned and measured and fitted for new clothes. Then there was tea with Lady Fanny, but both felt too tired and nervous to eat any of the tiny sandwiches or luscious cakes.

At last they were told that they might take a walk in the garden before dinner. They walked away from the house, sedately arm in arm, and then, as one, began to run as soon as they were out of sight of the house. They ended up, panting and breathless, in a little wood through which they could see the chimneys of the house next door.

"I don't know if I'll be able to take much of this," said Molly when they at last found a fallen log to sit on. "What say we write to Ma and ask her to fetch us home?"

"Oh, Molly," breathed Mary, "if only we *could*."

"Well, I don't see why not," said Molly bracingly. "It's like living with a sergeant major. I was so hungry at tea but she kept putting me off my food with her 'No, *no*! You must hold the teapot *so*.' And, ugh, that China tea. I'd have given anything for a really strong cup of coffee. I—"

She broke off, as a loud masculine voice could be heard from the garden next door. "Damn and blast this dead-alive hole," it said.

Both girls giggled nervously. "Let's go see," whispered Molly. "Sounds like a fellow spirit."

They got up and walked quietly through

the trees, over a springy carpeting of moss. A crumbling fern-covered stone wall marked the boundary between the Holdens' property and next door. A screen of trees blocked the view of the neighboring garden. Mary tugged at Molly's sleeve in a kind of pleading way but Molly was determined to have a look at this angry neighbor.

Pulling Mary behind her, she edged her way along the wall until she came to a gap in the trees. She found herself looking along a sort of narrow green tunnel of briars and bushes to a vista of cool lawns and garden chairs. One of the chairs suddenly went flying and there, in the gap, was the angry neighbor. He was a tall, swarthy, harsh-featured young man. His black slanting eyebrows under hair as thick and black as Molly's own gave him a Satanic look. He was wearing an old pair of riding breeches and an open-necked white shirt that accentuated his tan.

He was slashing at the bushes with a riding crop in a moody, vicious way.

Molly responded this time to Mary's tugging. Both turned and scampered back through the wood.

"Isn't he *terrible*," gasped Molly when they felt it safe to speak. "He looks like the devil!"

"Gels! Gels!" summoned an imperative voice from the house. Feeling as if they were back in school, the two sisters trudged toward the mansion.

Lady Fanny was dressed in a long velvet dinner gown, showing exactly the correct expanse of bosom in front and the correct amount of vertebrae behind.

"You are no longer schoolgirls," was her opening remark. "You are covered in bits of leaves. Retire to your rooms and change for dinner immediately. On second thought, perhaps you have nothing to change into. Get yourselves brushed up and don't be long. We dine in twenty minutes."

In less than the twenty minutes, the Maguires were timidly seated at an expanse of dining table and the nightmare began. "You must learn to take a little wine," ordered Lady Fanny. "Fill their glasses, James," she ordered a footman.

Mary rebelled. "I don't gotta take wine if'n I don't wanna."

Lady Fanny closed her eyes as if in pain. "This is going to be worse than I thought. You *must* have elocution lessons as soon as possible. Do *not* use double negatives, Mary. A little wine will do you no harm. No, Molly, one does *not* eat asparagus with a knife and fork. With the *fingers*, girl. The fingers."

Both girls occasionally looked toward Lord Toby. Several times he made a few deep rumblings as if indicating that he was about to erupt into speech, but each time Fanny quelled whatever it was he was about to say with one pale, cold eye.

Molly and Mary labored through exotic course after course, praying that each one might be the last. "Are you enjoying your first English dinner?" queried Lady Fanny.

"Sure. Swell," said Mary dreamily. The wine was going to her head.

"There will be *ready-made* clothes arriving for you on the morrow," said Lady Fanny. "These will have to do until your other clothes are ready. You must be prepared to change at least six times a day."

Molly choked on her food. "Six times!" she exclaimed in dismay. "That doesn't leave us time to do anything else."

"There will be *plenty* of time," retorted Lady Fanny. "You will be busy at first with your lessons. You must have elocution lessons. Not so much you, Molly. There is no harm in an American accent, in fact some gentlemen find it piquant, but Mary's grammar needs attention. Then you must have dancing lessons and lessons in deportment."

Molly made a bid for freedom. "I honestly don't think we're going to make it, Lady Fanny," she pleaded. "Why don't you just let us catch the next boat to Brooklyn?"

"Nonsense! You will like it well enough when you start going to balls and parties and see all the handsomest men in England falling at your feet."

It may have been the effect of the wine or it may just have been Molly's very feminine soul, but the thought of handsome Englishmen falling at her feet was suddenly infinitely appealing.

Anything further, however, that she might have wished to say was cut short by an appalled squawk from Lady Fanny. Mary had been eyeing a bowl of cool water in front of her plate. It looked very tempting, with little slivers of lemon floating in it. She raised it in both hands and took a deep drink.

"Good Heavens!" shrieked the appalled Lady Fanny. "Toby, do look! She drank from the finger bowl."

"So what!" muttered Mary dismally. "What a mazuma."

Lord Toby suddenly found his voice. "Leave 'em alone, Fanny. Give 'em time to run about a bit. Not much more than little gels, ain't they? Plenty of time for lessons."

"I don't know what you're butting in for," snapped Lady Fanny, but her husband held her glare without flinching. "Oh, very well. You may have a little holiday for the next few days. Get to know the place. Your parents are allowing you a very generous allowance. You will receive it from me each Monday morning."

Things began to look definitely brighter. Molly felt almost happy. Then she remembered the man next door and decided that it would be a useful way of turning the conversation away from themselves.

"That's a very angry-looking neighbor you have," she remarked.

"Which side?" asked Lord Toby, showing a spark of interest.

"The left."

"Oh, that must be poor Lord David Manley," sighed Fanny. "Nobody has seen him but he is supposed to be a very handsome man. And so rich! He contracted consumption, you know, and everyone thought he would die. But his doctor sent him to a sanatorium in Switzerland and he has been miraculously cured, they say. Poor boy. He bought the villa next door and is said to be convalescing."

"I don't think it could possibly have been Lord David," said Molly. "This man was very healthy and muscular and too harsh-featured to be called handsome."

"I believe his parents presented him with some sort of male nurse," said Lady Fanny. "That's probably who it was. Poor Lord David. He must still be very sickly."

41

A gentle snore and a small thump interrupted their conversation. Mary, overcome by the unaccustomed wine and masses of exotic food, had slowly slipped under the table and gone to sleep.

The following Sunday morning found the Maguire sisters to be the first members of the household awake. Breakfast, they remembered, was not until eleven o'clock. They would stroll down to the town and take a look around. Mary was complaining of a headache and Molly pointed out that fresh air would be just the thing to blow it away.

It was a pure, clear sunny morning. They walked down the drive, pushed open the great iron gates, and marched out into the road with a feeling of having escaped from prison.

They hesitated a little and then decided Hadsea must be on their left.

"Goddamnit, man," roared the well-remembered voice of the man who must be Lord David's nurse. "What the hell do you call this filth? I want coffee, good, strong dark coffee. Take this pap away and feed it to the cat." There was a sound of breaking china.

"Poor Lord David," murmured Molly. "Can you imagine how he must be bullied by that dreadful nurse?" She pictured a frail and beautiful aristocrat lying weakly on his sickbed, one blue-veined hand plucking restlessly at the covers, fair hair falling over a marble brow, as that angry voice ranted and raved.

The road led past the gardens of more enormous villas. All of them looked quite new. The air was heavy with the scent of roses and newly cut grass. Somewhere someone was frying bacon and the smell made the girls' stomachs rumble.

They turned a bend in the road and there was Hadsea. The little town was situated at the far end of a beautiful curve of sandy beach. With one accord, they raced along it.

The whole expanse of sea was the color of blue watered silk. Little pink shells studded the gleaming sand, bordered by golden clumps of broom. Lazy spirals of smoke rose from the chimneys of the town and in the distance they could faintly hear voices singing in the church. Lady Fanny had said nothing about going to church, which struck them as unusual. The fact was that Lady Fanny knew both girls to be Catholic and, being Anglican herself, had not known quite what to do with them. Hadsea did not boast a church that catered to such an unfashionable religion.

Soon they were walking along the deserted cobbled streets of the little town. All the shops were closed and shuttered.

"Well, at least we can find out where the post office is," said Molly. "And then we can post that letter to Mother as soon as we get our allowance, if things look too bad."

They wandered up one narrow lane and down another until Mary said, "Can *that* be it?"

Sure enough the sign above the door said clearly HADSEA GENERAL POST OFFICE. There was a small red stamp machine on a pedestal beside the door and on the pavement outside, a squat red pillar-box for posting letters, but there any resemblance to any sort of post office the girls had ever known ended. The window was full of buckets and spades, black sandshoes, jars of candy, balls of string, can openers, a picture of a lady in a diaphanous gown, who was staring disapprovingly at the Pyramids, a pair of whalebone corsets, and damp postcards showing sepia-tinted views of Hadsea.

"Do you think they'll actually get a letter from here to America?" said Molly, giggling. "Maybe they'll send it by bearer on a cleft stick."

Mary was about to reply when both girls suddenly heard the stifled sound of sobbing coming from somewhere at the rear of the building. Now, two well-bred English ladies would have walked on and minded their own business. But not the Maguire sisters.

They found a little passage at the side of the shop and walked along it toward the sound of the sobbing. It was coming from a small kitchen at the back. The girls stopped and looked at one another awkwardly. This was spying on someone's private grief. They were about to turn away when a rough voice stopped them in their tracks.

"Stop sniveling and hand over the money," it growled.

Molly threw her scruples to the winds and peered in a small window. A thin, frail, middle-aged woman was sitting at a scrubbed kitchen table with a money box open in front of her.

"I can't pay you any more," she was crying. "I've hardly got enough to eat."

"You'll pay me and you know why," growled her tormentor.

Molly squeezed her head around to bring him into view. He was a fat, pimply youth about her own age with brown greasy curls pasted to his low forehead. "How would you like the village to know you and your old man wasn't married? How would you like His Majesty's post office to know? Throw you out in the street, they would."

Still crying, the woman drew some notes and silver from the box and slowly laid them out on the table, where they were immediately snatched up. "This all?" he growled. "See you make it more next time or it'll be the worse for you."

As they heard him coming to the kitchen door, the Maguire sisters ran along the narrow passage and then stood staring in apparent fascination at the whalebone corsets. The burly youth strode past them.

"Let's follow him," hissed Molly.

The youth was keeping up a good pace but not once did he stop and look behind him. They followed him up through the streets, past the railway station, and along a narrow country lane. They kept well behind him, making sure that they only kept him in sight. A faint breeze had sprung up, bringing with it all the summer scents of the fields and the sea. The idyllic landscape made the squat figure in front of them strangely menacing. He at last stopped outside a small brick cottage on a rise, pushed open the door, and went in.

"Now we know where he lives. Back to the post office," said Molly.

Mary began to feel frightened. "Shouldn't we go to the police, Molly?" she asked timidly.

"No," said Molly. "Of course not. He would be arrested and then that poor woman's story

46

would come out in court and be all over the town newspaper."

At the post office the woman was still sitting at the table. Molly rapped on the window.

The woman looked up, startled, and then went to the kitchen door. The girls walked around to the back.

Her eyes still red with weeping, the woman introduced herself. "I am Mrs. Pomfret, the postmistress. I am afraid the post office is closed today. But if there is anything you need urgently . . ."

"We need to talk to you," said Molly firmly. "I reckon you could do with a little help. You see, we heard—"

Mrs. Pomfret blushed crimson, gasped, and then began to cry. Molly put an arm around the thin, shaking shoulders and drew her into the kitchen. "I'm going to make you a nice cup of tea and you're going to tell me all about it," she said firmly. "No one should have to keep that amount of trouble to themselves."

Glad of something ordinary to do, Mary took over and bustled about the stove preparing the tea. Molly sat down at the table and took Mrs. Pomfret's hand in her own. "Tell me about it," she said, her voice warm with sympathy.

Without knowing why she did it, Mrs. Pomfret found herself telling this strange American girl all about her trouble. Mr. Pomfret was dead. He had died of diphtheria two years ago. They both came from another town. Mr. Pomfret had not been free to marry her. His wife was a devout Roman Catholic and divorce was too expensive in any case. They had both decided to move away and start a new life together. Then Billy Barnstable had appeared upon the scene. Somehow he had ferreted out her secret and had started to blackmail her. If she lost her job as postmistress, she would be ruined. Did he live with his father and mother? No. He lodged with old Mr. Wothers who was as deaf as a post.

While the postmistress had been talking, Molly had been looking vaguely around the dark little kitchen. Her eyes alighted on a game rifle lying in one corner.

"Is that yours?" she asked.

Mrs. Pomfret stared. "It was Mister Pomfret's," she said sadly. "Used it for shooting rabbits, he did. Not that I know anything about guns."

"Have you any cartridges?"

"Well now," said Mrs. Pomfret in surprise. "The things you ask! Yes, dear, there's a box of them nasty things on the mantelshelf."

Molly looked at them carefully. "If you would lend me this gun this evening after dark,

I think . . . I just think . . . I could put an end to your troubles."

"Here now!" exclaimed the postmistress in alarm. "This isn't the wild West."

"Trust me," said Molly gently. "Just trust me. . . ."

CHAPTER THREE

Mary was shivering with fear. Molly was excited. The hour was eleven o'clock. They had managed to creep out of the Holden mansion without being observed.

As they hurried along the sandy beach to Hadsea, Molly reflected that this was surely much more exciting than a London Season. Even more exciting than meeting King Edward himself!

Mary felt that her adored sister was making some dreadful mistake. Both were huddled in long plaid capes over their school dresses. It was a bright moonlit night and the sea spread out to their left like a sheet of silver, the only sound in the quiet night being the soft sibilant whispering of the tiny waves on the beach.

The warm glow from an oil lamp lit up the kitchen at the back of the post office. The postmistress was nervously waiting for them.

"I must be mad," she whispered, handing Molly the gun. She watched in amazement as Molly expertly snapped it open and began loading it with a practiced hand. "What if Constable Jenkins should see you?" Mr. Jenkins was the town policeman.

"Don't worry," said Molly with a grin. "There isn't going to be anyone awake but us."

Both girls whispered their good-byes. Molly hid the gun under her long cape and they sped silently along the narrow lanes that led out of the town. All too soon for Mary, Mr. Wothers's small brick cottage appeared on the rise, silhouetted against the moon.

Molly felt Mary's arm tremble against her own. She should have persuaded her young sister to stay behind. But it was too late now. May as well get on with it. Mrs. Pomfret had said that Mr. Wothers was stone-deaf. Molly fervently hoped this was the case and that the repulsive Billy Barnstable would answer the door himself. Suddenly feeling as nervous as Mary and hoping that Barnstable did not keep a dog, Molly raised her hand and rapped firmly on the kitchen door at the back of the house. The front door looked as if it hadn't been opened in years.

There was a long silence. Molly rapped again. The yellow light of a candle flame sprang up in one of the upstairs rooms and shortly afterward the light disappeared and reappeared in the kitchen downstairs. There was the sound of bolts being drawn back. The door opened, and Billy Barnstable stood looking at them, his nightshirt stuffed into his trousers. "What you want?" he demanded, and then gave a cavernous yawn.

"We want you to stop blackmailing Mrs. Pomfret," said Molly.

Billy Barnstable held up the candle and looked at the girls in its flickering light. An unlovely smile creased his fat features. "You're nuthin' but a couple o' kids," he laughed. "Get back to your ma and stop pokin' your noses in where they don't belong."

"All right," said Molly angrily. "I am no longer *asking* you to stop blackmailing Mrs. Pomfret. I'm *telling* you."

Molly backed away from the kitchen door into the garden as she spoke, with Mary hiding behind her. Billy's smile grew even broader. He thought Molly was frightened and strolled after her into the garden.

"An' who's going to stop me? You?" And he gave a great fat laugh.

53

"Yes, me. Me and this," said Molly. She took out the rifle from under her coat and leveled it straight at Billy. "No one knows we're here," she said in a voice like ice. "I can put a bullet through your fat heart and no one would be any the wiser. And if you do not leave Mrs. Pomfret alone, that is exactly what I *shall* do."

Billy quickly recovered from his initial fright at the sight of the gun. "Don't try to scare me, missy. You don't know one end o' that thing from the other."

Molly backed against the garden wall, as far away from Billy as she could get. Then she raised the rifle. There was a loud report and the candle went out. Billy realized with horror that she had neatly shot out the flame.

"Still not convinced?" the dreadful girl went on.

She saw in the bright moonlight a rusty can on top of a fence post in the adjoining field. Again that wicked-looking gun went up. *Bang!* And the can spun from the top of the post and fell to the grass. It was the shot of a true marksman.

Billy was now well and truly frightened. The only things he ever read were penny dreadfuls, which regularly featured stories of the wild West, where people went around shooting their neighbors with simply horrible abandon. He realized with a shock that this girl was American, the spitting image of Deirdre of Dead Man's Gulch in his latest story.

"I'll tell the perleece on you," he whimpered.

"Oh, no you won't," said Molly. "Or I'll have you dragged off to court for blackmailing. And don't dare even poke your ugly nose into that post office to buy a stamp. You're a farm laborer, aren't you? Well, just remember, I can pick you off as you work in the fields. Think of that, Master Billy. Think of it every time you bend over."

The unnatural girl gave an awful laugh.

Billy cringed even more. "Look, missy, it was a bit of a joke, like. I never meant to do any harm."

"Starving an old lady out of her income is criminal," said Molly. "Which reminds me. Get up those stairs and bring down any money you have, and if I think it's not enough, I shall shoot you first in one knee cap and then in the other until you produce the goods."

Billy fled and returned, gasping and sweating, with a dirty tin box. There seemed to be quite a lot of money in it.

"Thank you," she said sweetly. "If I were you, Master Billy, I would find a job in some other town. You'll get out of this town if you know what's good for you. Now, skedaddle!"

Billy needed no second bidding. That "get

out of town" rang in his ears with a familiar sound. That was what Deirdre of Dead Man's Gulch had said to the rustler. Sweating with fear, he climbed the stairs to his small attic to begin packing up his belongings.

Mary and Molly walked off, triumphant. Mary was desperately trying to stifle a nervous fit of the giggles without much success. "Oh, did you see his face, Molly, when you shot out the candle? I felt almost sorry for him."

"I hate bullies," said Molly roundly. "This is much more worthwhile than parading around in dresses and learning to speak as if we've got mouths full of rocks. And that reminds me —talking of bullies—we must do something about that dreadful nurse of Lord David's. Soon as we get our allowance tomorrow, we'll buy us some goodies suitable for an invalid and take them 'round. 'Course we won't say anything to Lady Fanny. 'It is not *at all* the thing for a young lady to approach any gentleman to whom she has not been introduced,'" she mimicked.

When they reached the post office, Mrs. Pomfret was waiting, trembling, on the kitchen doorstep. She could hardly believe her ears at their news. Billy leaving town! She would have given Molly all the recovered money if she could. But Molly would not hear of it.

Mrs. Pomfret, she said, had supplied some excitement in this dead-alive hole.

Molly wondered where she had heard that phrase before and then remembered the male nurse. Now, there was a bully worthy of Molly Maguire's steel. She could hardly wait for the morrow.

Lord David Manley was halfway down the brandy decanter and feeling no pain. He had returned that evening from a visit to the hospital in Southampton and his lungs had been pronounced in good shape. With great daring, he lit a forbidden cheroot and settled back in the chair.

Now that he didn't have to stay in it any longer, Hadsea didn't seem such a bad place. Of course he had had to keep the usual matchmaking mamas and their damned invitations at bay. He had had, as usual, to cope with various county maidens whose bicycles, automobiles, or carriages had conveniently broken down outside his door. But that happened with boring regularity in London as well.

It had been a long time since he had believed that a woman could love him for himself alone and not for his well-known fortune. As far as the fair sex was concerned, he thought cynically, it was easier to pay for one's pleasures.

But it was about time he set up his nursery. Lady Cynthia Whitworth would fill the bill admirably. She came from good old stock, was highly decorative, and acidulous and witty enough to retain a good deal of his tepid interest.

She had sensibly pointed out to him that there was no point in getting wed if he had tuberculosis. This might have seemed cold-hearted to a less cynical man but the jaundiced Lord David found it an eminently practical point of view. He would write to her on the morrow and tell her his good news.

In a fit of remorse for his previous ill-temper, he had given his servants the evening off and a small bonus each to go and drink to his restored health. Now he was simply enjoying the rare pleasure of getting comfortably drunk.

A soft English twilight was visible through the open windows. The air was heavy with the scent of leaves and grass and flowers. Somewhere in the garden a nightingale sang and the leaves of the old trees on the dew-laden lawns rustled and whispered in the lightest of evening breezes. And he was a whole man again. His constant companion, the specter of death and disease, had fled.

He stretched out his long, muscular legs, encased in an old pair of flannels, and breathed a sigh of pure contentment.

The clanging of the doorbell jarred through the evening air like the obscenity that rose to Lord David's lips. He waited for his butler to answer it and get rid of whoever it was and then realized that he had given the servants the night off. With another curse he got somewhat unsteadily to his feet and walked through the hall and jerked open the door.

Two schoolgirls dressed in shabby plaid dresses and dowdy dark-brown felt hats stood looking at him in the failing light. One was holding a basket with a checkered cloth over it.

They must be collecting for some local charity, he decided.

"Come into the study," he said abruptly and turned and walked away without looking to see if they were following him.

He sat down at his desk and drew out his checkbook. He looked up. Both girls were standing in front of him, looking at him with unnerving wide-eyed stares.

"How much?" said Lord David, his head bent over his checkbook, his pen poised.

"I don't know what you mean," said the taller of the girls. Her voice had a transatlantic twang and Lord David looked up in surprise.

"Haven't you come to ask for a donation to something?" His light, pleasant voice was only slightly slurred.

"We've come to see Lord David," said the elder firmly. "We have brought him a basket of nourishing food because we heard he was ill. So if you will just announce us, my good man . . ."

Lord David got to his feet, his face set in an unpleasant sneer.

He realized that the girls were slightly older than he had first thought . . . about seventeen and eighteen, he judged. It seemed that not only was his privacy to be broken by the local debutantes but by the village maidens as well!

"Very clever," he said. "Very, very clever. Are you sure you haven't sprained your ankles or something? The intrigues you young girls get up to in the hope of marrying a fortune amazes me. You will find the door still open. Close it behind you when you get out and take that basket of . . . of . . . codswallop with you."

"We demand to see Lord David," said Molly haughtily. "I did not come here to bandy words with his male nurse."

"Male nurse? You impertinent baggage!" said Lord David wrathfully. "Male nurse? If you mean that mentally muscle-bound idiot my parents sent me, I sacked him weeks ago. *I*, dear girl, am Lord David!"

For one long minute the elder girl looked at him with those astonishing blue eyes.

"Bully," said Miss Molly Maguire, "for you. Because of your nasty common behavior, we thought *you* were the nurse. You, Lord David! You're nothing but a nasty old cheese. I wouldn't cross the street to help you if you were dying. If you're an example of an English aristocrat—one of those yobs we're supposed to marry—we'd be a damn sight better off with the boys in Brooklyn."

"Molly!" pleaded Mary, tugging at her arm, her large eyes filled with tears. But the sight of her little sister's distress fanned the flames of Molly's wrath.

"As for money," she went on, "we're both stinking rich. If you've got girls running after you for your money, then take my advice and marry one of them. No girl is going to marry an ugly-looking cuss like you for any other reason."

"How dare you!" yelled Lord David.

Picking up her basket and taking her young sister by the arm, Molly marched to the threshold and then turned and looked back to where Lord David stood smoldering behind his desk.

"I shall find out where your parents live," grated Lord David, "and make sure that for your impertinence you both get the spanking you richly deserve."

The elder girl's eyes raked over him with

contempt, from his shabby flannels to his venerable blazer and open-necked shirt.

"Aw! Stuff it, your lordship," said Miss Molly Maguire.

The door banged behind her with such force that the whole house shook.

CHAPTER FOUR

The Maguire sisters sat bolt upright in Lady
Fanny's open brougham. They could not in
fact do anything else, since their new corsets
had them strapped into a rigid position. Both
were dressed in blonde lace tea gowns, Molly's
threaded with scarlet ribbon and Mary's with
blue. Both wore large picture hats embellished
with fruit and roses. Their glossy hair had
been put up for the first time.

The girls had just completed their first social engagement, a garden party at the rec-
tory, which Lady Fanny had felt would not
be too demanding for their first occasion. Lady
Fanny had developed a headache at the last
moment so the girls had been sent on their

own with a list of instructions. They were to confine their conversation to yes and no. Mary was not to slurp her tea or get crumbs on her dress. If pressed, they might converse about the weather. On *no account* must they ever mention that dreadful Maguire's Leprechaun Dew. Let people assume their family fortune came from some respectable American business like railroads, or "Daddy made a killing on Wall Street."

The girls had followed her instructions to the letter. Both were feeling exhausted after the stifling discomfort of new clothes and new corsets. It *had* been pleasant, however, to receive the attentions of various young men. But now both longed to get home and change into something more comfortable.

With their parasols held at exactly the correct angle, they clopped through the streets of Hadsea, pleasurably aware of the admiring attention of the townspeople.

They were just on the outskirts of the town, when Molly's sharp ears picked up the sounds of children crying. She called to the driver to stop. The sounds were coming from a small alley. At the far end a thick-set youth was twisting the arms of two smaller boys—twins, by the look of them—and to Molly's horror, the tearful smaller children put their hands in their pockets and handed over a penny each to the older boy.

"This place is *crawling* with bullies," cried Molly. "Coachman. Go and punch that older boy's head and give those little children their money back!"

"It's not my place to interfere, miss," said the coachman, turning around with an impertinent grin on his face. "Boys will be boys, I allus say."

"Ooooh!" cried Molly in a rage. She jumped down from the carriage and marched up the alley.

"Here, you," she cried to the older boy. "What do you mean by taking money from these children?"

The older boy looked at her, found he was the same size, and remarked in a cheeky whine, "Mind yer own business."

Molly looked down at the twins, who were regarding her with admiration. "What are your names, my dears?"

"Please miss, I'm Bobby and that there's me brother, Jim, and that big bully is Harry Petts. He's always a-takin' our pocket money, miss, and 'e says 'e'll beat us if we tell Mum."

Molly turned and faced Harry Petts. "Give them their money back," she ordered.

The youth grinned, looked down the alley

and noticed that the coachman was going to do nothing about it, and said, "And who's going to make me?"

"I am," said Molly simply. "Put up your dukes."

Harry looked at her clenched fists and let out a guffaw. This was great sport. "Come on then," he laughed, licking his thumb.

Now, Molly had learned to fight the hard way in the playgrounds of Brooklyn, but for a moment she had forgotten the art, and a well-aimed punch from Harry landed right in her eye. Molly drew back and Harry laughed with glee, thinking she was going to turn and run.

Memory flooded back. Molly's hands were still hard and callused from housekeeping and shop work.

Miss Molly Maguire brought a haymaker up from the ground and Harry Petts collapsed on the cobbles.

"Good-oh!" cheered Mary, who had rushed up to help. "That showed him. Ain't you the greatest, Molly." Molly raised her arms in a triumphant boxer's salute and then froze. Standing at the end of the alley and staring at her with amused interest was none other than Lord David Manley.

Molly was suddenly aware that her hair was coming down at the back, that her hat was askew, and that, from the throbbing in her right eye, she was about to develop the shiner of all time.

Lord David strode forward to meet her. Molly blinked slightly at the impact of his charming smile. His hand was outstretched.

"By Jove, ma'am," he cried. "That was a great hit!"

To his surprise, the strange girl ignored his outstretched hand. "Did you just stand there watching like a great palooka?" she said scornfully. "Seems to me you Englishmen are a spineless lot. Here, boys!" The twins came running up like eager puppies and stared at their rescuer with worshipful admiration. Molly pulled out her purse and selected a few pennies. "Go buy yourselves some candy."

"Candy, miss?"

"Allow me to translate," said Lord David in a cold voice. He had recognized in the smartly dressed young lady the schoolgirl who had so freely insulted him in his own study. "The lady means sweeties."

"Oh, miss," said Bobby. "Thanks ever so. If 'n ever you need help, miss, you just call on us."

"I will, indeed," laughed Molly, still ignoring Lord David. "Come, Mary."

Mary climbed into the carriage after her sister, her face averted from Lord David.

Miss Molly Maguire leaned back in the carriage and unfurled her lacy parasol. Lord David was tall and, even though she was seated in the high-sprung open carriage, Molly saw through the lace of her parasol that Lord David's tanned face was on a level with her own. She thought privately that he was looking very handsome indeed. His gray suit had been tailored by the hand of a master and his tall silk hat accentuated his height. She felt irrationally angry at the little twinge of attraction she suddenly experienced for this man. She lowered her parasol. She smiled sweetly at his lordship. In impeccable upper-class English accents Miss Molly Maguire said, "So long . . . *buster!*"

The carriage bowled off, leaving Lord David staring after it.

The twins took one look at his angry face and then down the alley to where Harry Petts was struggling to his feet and took to their heels.

Harry Petts stumbled toward Lord David. "If I get me 'ands on 'er, I'll wring 'er neck, that I will," he was muttering. Lord David barred his way.

"You obviously have not learned your lesson, laddie," he said in his light, pleasant voice. "If I catch you bullying again, then you will have me to deal with."

Harry stared in awe at Lord David, from his polished boots to the top of his silk hat, and cringed back against the wall of the alley. Keeping his eyes fixed on his new adversary, he edged his shoulders around the corner, and then turned and ran as hard as he could.

Lord David began to walk toward his home, following the direction that Molly's carriage had taken. He was furious with that cheeky girl. How dare she! Who was this little upstart American who looked at London's biggest marriage prize as if he were something lying in the gutter?

It was just as well that he was shaking the dust of Hadsea from his polished heels. He need never see her again. Now . . . just why was that thought so depressing? Why should he calmly walk off and leave that cheeky girl to have the last word? He was well aware of his powers of attraction. Then he should have his revenge. He would have that little American trembling breathlessly in his arms before the month was out. But how to break down her guard? He needed an ally. Then he remembered Roderick, Marquess of Leamouth. Roddy, with his engaging ways, his mop of golden curls, and his Greek profile. Roddy, who could charm the heart of the most bitter dowager. That was it! Roddy would court the young one and he the older. And what girls in the whole of the British Empire could stand an onslaught like that?

Several days of elocution lessons, dancing lessons, deportment lessons, and dress fittings had passed. The glorious sunset that was Molly's eye was fading nicely.

The next event on the girls' social calendar seemed a simple one. They were to stand behind Lady Fanny on a makeshift platform in Hadsea High Street and watch her take the salute as the local Boy Scout troop marched past. Then when she handed prizes for merit to deserving boys, they were to hand her the appropriate books. Nothing could be simpler.

The girls looked as cool and pretty as salads in organza dresses of palest green and large, shady straw hats bound with wide silk ribbons of the same color.

Lady Fanny looked impressive in an afternoon suit of white raw silk that she had had designed especially for the occasion. It had military epaulets in gold and scarlet silk and the bosom of her long, straight jacket was embellished by crossed gold cords. Her long skirt, hobbled in the latest fashion, had seemed so divine on the models in the showroom but now seemed to be in danger of bursting at the seams under the pressure of Lady Fanny's mannish strides.

The girls were sitting primly on the sofa in the drawing room while Lady Fanny rehearsed her speech.

"My lords, ladies and—*cough, cough*—gentlemen . . . Oh, dear, I *would* get a cough at a time like this. What—*cough, cough, garrrh*—am I to—*cough*—do? It is nearly time to go."

Molly looked at Mary and Mary looked at Molly.

"I know you said we weren't to mention it," said Molly, "but you *have* got a terrible cough and we have got a bottle of Maguires' Leprechaun Dew in our trunk upstairs."

"I'll—*cough*—try *anything*," said Lady Fanny weakly.

Molly reappeared a few minutes later, holding a bottle. The leprechaun looked evilly at Lady Fanny and Lady Fanny looked doubtfully back. She was about to refuse when she was overtaken by another fit of coughing. She looked at her reflection in the mirror and straightened her smart military shako. She *must* be all right for the parade. Lady Ann Abbott, her dearest rival, was to be present. She picked up the bottle of Maguires' Leprechaun Dew and after eyeing it for a few seconds with all the enthusiasm of Juliet viewing

71

Friar Lawrence's phial, she swallowed half the contents.

"Dear, goodness me!" she exclaimed. "That was unexpectedly pleasant. Come, girls, let us go. Chins up and best foots forward . . . I mean feets . . . feet. Oh, dear!" she ended with a surprisingly girlish giggle. "I feel simply marvelous."

Molly stood nervously behind Lady Fanny on the rostrum and wondered what to do. Should she risk the Maguire fortunes by informing Lady Fanny that Maguires' Leprechaun Dew was 140 proof? Surely they had enough money already. Lady Fanny was sitting with her hands on her knees and a vacant smile on her face, rather like the end man at a minstrel show waiting for Rastus to elucidate.

Molly took a tentative step forward. But it was then that she heard the first strains of the band. Molly cried listening to bands the way other women cry at weddings. To her, the sound of a marching band was all the essence of lost summers and lost childhood rolled into one. Lady Fanny, the rostrum, the dignitaries, the mayor, the Boy Scouts, and Hadsea all faded away to be replaced by the smells and noises of childhood New York. Her ears rang with the rattle of the elevated trains, the shrill cries of the street vendors, the fox-trots of the forties, and the shrill squeals of her friends of the Brooklyn playgrounds. Molly Maguire stood with a lump in her throat and the tears of homesickness rolling down her cheeks, unaware that Lady Fanny had risen to her feet and, instead of taking the salute, was waving merrily and shouting "coo-ee" to the ranks of startled Boy Scouts.

Molly recovered just as the first scout mounted the platform to receive his prize. "James Benson," she whispered in Lady Fanny's ear. "Prize for tracking."

"Darling, darling, boy," cooed Lady Fanny, stroking the startled Boy Scout's arm. He was a tall, attractive-looking boy with an unruly thatch of thick brown hair. Lady Fanny's hand had moved from his arm and was now tenderly ruffling James's hair. "We won a prize for tracking, did we?" she murmured. "Such a dear, clever boy." James Benson retreated hurriedly and almost fell down the steps. "Next!" shouted Lady Fanny with a joyful, predatory eye. There was an anxious rustling movement among the dignitaries. All was not well. Lady Fanny Holden, the model of upright behavior and strict discipline, was behaving very strangely indeed.

Molly felt that she must do something, but

Mary was already handing Lady Fanny the next prize and murmuring, "Joseph Willicombe, sports prize."

Joseph was the smallest of the scouts, with a face like a cherub. He had rosy cheeks and black curly hair and a surprisingly red and sensuous mouth for one so young.

"My dear boy," trilled Lady Fanny. "And you are our best at sports. And so small. Are you *small*, boy?"

"Yes, my lady. Please, my lady," said Joseph with wide-eyed wonder.

"Marvelous," breathed Lady Fanny, staring at Joseph's red mouth. "Now, Joseph, you will give Lady Fanny a nice big kiss, won't you?"

The boy looked wildly around at his scout master for help but the scout master's face was like wood. Lady Fanny swooped down and kissed the horribly embarrassed boy on the mouth.

A ripple of shock ran through the crowd. Lady Ann Abbott gave tongue. "What's the matter with you, Fanny?" she hissed.

"Nothing," said Lady Fanny, turning one pale, cold eye on her rival. "You're just jealous because of my smart suit." This was said in such accents of concentrated venom that the rest of the dignitaries could not find the courage to stop her ladyship. But Lady Fanny's pink cloud had dwindled away, leaving her with a nagging ache behind the eyes and a sudden hatred of the whole world.

A small, thin, cross-eyed scout was standing waiting. "Henry Beddings. Fire-making," said Molly desperately.

Lady Fanny stared down at the scout with hatred. "Fire-making!" she exclaimed bitterly. "Of all the stupid things to give a prize for. I know you. You're the one who tried to set fire to my hedge last autumn. I'll fire-make you, you little pyromaniac." She tried to swipe Henry with his prize and missed. The boy scuttled down from the platform, and Lady Fanny threw his prize after him. Then suddenly feeling very weak, she collapsed into her chair and fell sound asleep.

Molly realized that she must do something to save Lady Fanny's reputation. She moved quickly to the front of the platform.

"My lords, ladies, and gentlemen," she cried. The unexpected American accents caught everyone's attention. "Lady Holden is suffering from a very bad cough. She should have stayed in bed. But she is very conscious of her duty and took some very strong medicine so that she would be able to perform the prize-giving. The medicine is extremely strong and, as you can see, Lady Holden is suffering from its effects. It takes great dedication to duty and to the welfare of Hadsea to attempt to speak despite the influence of a strong drug. I suggest we give three hearty cheers for Lady Holden."

Molly had never looked more beautiful. The crowd, glad to have a little excitement, and the dignitaries, glad to be relieved of embarrassment, cheered wildly.

Molly held up her hands for silence. "And now," she cried, "I would like James Benson, Joseph Willicombe, and Henry Beddings to receive three cheers for behaving like true Boy Scouts in unusual and embarrassing circumstances." More wild cheers.

Then Molly delivered her master stroke. "We are, however, fortunate in having with us today Lady Holden's dear friend who, I feel sure, will be glad to stand in for her. Lady Ann Abbott."

Lady Ann Abbott sailed to the front of the platform, her bosom heaving with gratification. She pulled down the front of her sensible tweed jacket, casting a pitying look at her fallen rival. She, Ann, had been looking forward to telling Fanny exactly how badly she, Fanny, had behaved. But enough was enough. Lady Abbott was having her moment of triumph and could afford to be magnanimous. Poor, dear Fanny should never hear of her disgrace from *her*. Which was exactly what the clever Miss Molly Maguire had planned.

Lord David and his friend, Roddy, Marquess of Leamouth, walked thoughtfully away from the prize-giving.

"She's divine, you know. Absolutely divine," said Roddy. "I wouldn't do anything to upset her for the world."

"She's a militant baggage," snapped Lord David. "Didn't you see the way she stood up and made that speech? Not a feminine nerve in her whole body."

"Oh, not *that* one," said Roddy. "Her sister. The quiet one who stood at the back. What's her name?"

"Mary," replied Lord David, who had made it his business to find out as much as possible about the Maguire sisters.

"Mary," breathed Roddy.

Lord David smiled at him indulgently. "You're always falling head over heels in love with unsuitable females."

"This one's not unsuitable," said Roddy. "She's an angel."

"An angel who sounds as if she hailed from one of the less salubrious parts of New York," said his friend dryly.

"Snob," said Roddy, turning back for a last look at Mary. "I'll lay siege to Miss Mary Maguire, David, but my intentions will be honorable."

Lord David smiled to himself. Roddy's intentions were *always* honorable. That was part of his charm.

"And," Roddy was going on, "when do we get a chance to get close to the girls?"

"After today," replied Lord David, "I think that Lady Ann will send them a hurried last-minute invitation to her daughter's ball. She had no intention of asking them, you know, but after Miss Molly's performance today I have no doubt she will be all over them."

Roddy looked slyly at his friend. "Don't you think you're going to have a bit of a hard time with the fair Molly?"

"Oh, she'll come around," said his lordship with maddening assurance. "I've never had any difficulty before."

CHAPTER FIVE

Despite all his much-vaunted assurance, Lord David found himself strangely nervous as he stood at the edge of the Abbotts' ballroom and waited for the arrival of the Maguire sisters.

The long French windows of the ballroom were open onto the gardens. Brightly colored lanterns were strung through the trees. Vincent and His Melody Makers, specially imported from London, were playing a Viennese waltz with gusto. Great banks of hothouse flowers bloomed against the walls of the ballroom. All the most elegant members of the county were present and even a few sprigs of the nobility had traveled in from other summer parts, drawn by Lady Ann's well-deserved reputation for lavish hospitality.

The band hit a triumphant last chord and the voice of the majordomo could be heard announcing, "Miss Molly Maguire and Miss Mary Maguire." He looked eagerly around.

The Maguire sisters were coming slowly down the red-carpeted stairs. They were dressed in ball gowns of white and silver gauze, and real white rosebuds were threaded through the glossy black curls of their hair. With their startling blue eyes, creamy complexions, and high cheekbones, they looked strangely exotic —two foreign birds come to ruffle the plumage of the gray English doves. They made every other woman look colorless.

Roddy was already hurrying to the foot of the stairs to meet them. Lord Toby and Lady Fanny followed behind. Lady Fanny was wearing a ball gown of heavy crimson satin, which vaguely hinted at military discipline by having things like epaulets on the hips. She carried a lorgnette with a very long handle, which she brandished like a swagger stick, and her feathered headdress suggested more the scarlet crest of a warlike Roman than a feminine adornment for the dance.

For once, however, Fanny was looking as hunted as her husband. She could not remember one thing about the prize-giving, although everyone had informed her in such *kind* and sympathetic tones that she had done very well.

Lady Ann had been particularly sugary. Lady Fanny had been on the point of refusing the invitation to the ball but the stupendous news that none other than Lord David Manley was to be present had forced her to change her mind. The Maguire girls were looking enchanting and Lady Fanny knew where her duty lay. If only Molly would curb her sense of humor and if only Mary would learn to keep her mouth shut, then they might be married before the summer ended. Mary had quickly adopted the English accent and manners of the aristocracy but the context of her conversation was still pure Brooklynese.

Roddy gloomily retired from the Maguires' crowd of admirers. "I only managed to get two dances," he said to Lord David. "All these other damned chappies are scribbling away in the girls' dance cards. How did you get on?"

"Not any better than you," said Lord David. "Don't worry. I have a plan. Before the next dance starts, plunge in there, laddie, and ask to see their dance cards. Tease, you know. Say you can't believe they're fully booked. Make a note in that brain of yours of the names of the chappies who have them signed up for the supper dance. Then we'll take it from there."

The marquess plunged back into the crowd

of admirers. He started chatting and laughing. Lord David noticed that Mary looked at the marquess with glowing eyes and that Molly was even smiling at him with open friendliness. The young Americans had not yet learned to school their expressions.

Vincent and His Melody Makers struck up once again and Lord David was joined by Roddy. "Cuthbert Postlethwaite has got yours," he said, "and Alfred Bingham has mine."

"Oh, good," said Lord David matter-of-factly. "I hate Postlethwaite. I'll go and get rid of him directly."

"Hey, what about me?" cried Roddy. "I like old Bingham."

"Appeal to his better nature," laughed Lord David, striding off.

Refreshments were being served under various marquees on the lawns. Beneath one, draped inside in great swathes of pink silk, only champagne was being served, and it was into this one that Lord David saw Cuthbert Postlethwaite's broad back disappearing.

Cuthbert had his large face in a silver tankard. Lord David slapped him heartily on the back and said cheerfully, "And how are you, you silly little man?"

"Quite well, you old turd," said Cuthbert amiably. Ladies were not present.

"Last time I saw you was at Cannes," said

Lord David, staring at Cuthbert's frilled shirt. "That gigolo at the hotel must have been a damned decent chap."

"Why?"

"I see he gave you his shirt," said Lord David, helping himself to champagne.

Cuthbert's broad face became puce. "If your lungs weren't rotting in your chest, you'd answer for that," he said wrathfully.

"I got the all clear from the hospital. Everyone knows that," said Lord David. "Of course, a lot of chaps pretend not to know it. You know the sort. Frightened they'll get hurt."

Cuthbert was smaller in height than Lord David but he was powerfully built. He put down his tankard and stared at his lordship in blank amazement.

"Are you calling me a c-coward?" he stammered.

"Y-yes," mimicked Lord David. "I am calling you a c-coward."

"Outside," said Cuthbert. "I've wanted to smash your face in for years and now I'm going to do it."

They marched outside the tent and into the shrubbery while the band played on.

Molly swayed elegantly in the arms of her partner and assured herself that she was glad that that horrible Lord David had chosen to disappear. Perhaps he would stay away and not turn up to claim his two dances after supper. She was conscious of a faint sinking feeling in the pit of her stomach. She put it down to worrying about her sister. Mary was floating in Roddy's arms, looking like a child at Christmas. Molly distrusted Roddy. First, of course, because of his friendship with Lord David. Secondly, because he seemed somehow insincere. It was rather like watching someone flirting in a play, Molly decided.

She whirled to a stop and gave her partner an abstracted smile and refused his offer of refreshment. She wandered over in the direction of the chaperons, meaning to have a word with Lady Fanny. Then she saw a young girl sitting forlornly on her own beside a pillar. She was dressed in a very dashing Paris gown that was much too old for her and much too daring for her obviously retiring manner. She had a very young, freckled face that bore the traces of tears. Molly's warm heart was touched. She plumped herself down beside the girl, ignoring the fact that her next partner would be searching for her, and asked, sympathetically, "Are you all right?"

"Yes, thank you," said the girl in a faint voice.

"I guess we haven't been introduced, and

you British set such store by introductions so I'll introduce myself. I'm Molly Maguire, and the one out on the floor that looks like me is my sister, Mary."

"I know who you are," said the girl in a low voice. "*He's* done nothing but look at you all evening."

"He? Who?" asked Molly somewhat incoherently.

"Lord David."

"That bully," scoffed Molly. "Oh, here, for land sakes don't start crying again. Tell me all about it. Start by telling me your name. Come on. I'm not going to eat you."

"My name is Jennifer Strange," said the girl, speaking in such a low whisper that Molly had to bend to hear. "I have been sent down here to stay with my Aunt Matilda, only because Lord David is here. My—my mother is very ambitious and—and—persuaded my aunt that there was a good chance of me marrying Lord David so they bought me a dashing new wardrobe and—and—sent me here—and—and he won't even l-look at me."

"But your mother can't *force* you to marry just anyone," exclaimed Molly.

"N-no one is f-forcing me," said Jennifer, hiccuping. "I *love* him. He's s-so strong and masterful."

At first Molly thought this a bit theatrical

but then she put it down to the British attitude.

"Well, you won't attract his attention sitting behind this pillar," Molly couldn't help pointing out.

"H-he won't even see me with you and your sister around. And—and—my aunt's so furious, I'm hiding from her."

Another bully! Another dragon to fight. Molly's blue eyes gleamed. "You just relax," she said, laying a comforting hand on the girl's knee. "Leave everything to Molly."

Jennifer raised adoring eyes to this new, strong personality in her life. Molly smiled down at her. She was really very engaging. Rather like a small Pekingese. Resisting an impulse to pat her on the head, Molly returned to the floor just as the supper dance was being announced and found herself looking up into the tanned and somewhat battered features of Lord David.

She forgot her dislike of him as she stared at his face. "You look as if you have been in a prize fight," she exclaimed as he led her unresistingly into the steps of the waltz. And then, "Say, isn't this someone else's dance?" She tried to tug her hand free to look at her dance card but he kept her hand in a strong clasp.

"I wouldn't worry about it if I were you,"

he murmured. "It was Cuthbert's dance, but he . . . er . . . met with an accident in the grounds and had to go home."

"Ran into a fist, by the look of things," said Miss Maguire with an irritating lack of femininity.

Lord David decided to ignore the remark. Instead he smiled down into her eyes and tightened his grip around her slim waist. "You know you really are a most beautiful girl," he said.

Molly felt that something odd was happening to her breath. It must be because he was holding her so tightly. She also felt as if she had just been filleted. Her body seemed to be boneless as it automatically followed his every movement. They danced in silence, but Molly felt that this disturbing man was making love to her without opening his mouth. She was glad when the dance finally ended and they walked out into the garden toward the marquee that held the supper tables.

"And how do you find England?" asked Lord David, when they were finally seated.

"I only know this part," said Molly. "Well, it's quaint and kinda pretty. Everything's so small. Small cottages, small fields, and then after you stay for a bit it seems to get bigger and bigger."

"You must be expanding the horizons of

your mind," teased Lord David, helping her to lobster patties. "For Heaven's sake, don't gulp your champagne like that. It isn't lemonade. You're too young to know what strange things too much alcohol can make respectable people do!"

Molly suddenly thought of Lady Fanny as she had appeared at the prize-giving under the influence of Maguires' Leprechaun Dew and blushed.

"Oh, so you *do* know," teased Lord David, appreciatively eyeing the blush. "Now, I wonder why."

Molly racked her brains for some way to change the subject and then remembered poor Jennifer.

"Do you ever dance with wallflowers?" she asked abruptly. His slanting brows almost vanished into his black hair.

"Do I *what*?"

"You heard me. Do you dance with wallflowers?"

"No, I don't, you strange girl," he said. "And if I did," he added with simple arrogance, "then that girl would not be a wallflower much longer."

"Why?"

"Because I set the fashion."

"Oh!" said Molly, looking at him thoughtfully. "Say, do you feel like doing me a favor?"

"Anything," he replied.

"Then, lemme see," said Molly, looking in her dance card.

"Your English accent is slipping," he murmured.

Molly chose to ignore his remark. "I have promised you two dances in the second half of the gig. Okay?"

"Okay," repeated his lordship politely.

"Well, see here," said Molly, putting her gloved elbows on the table and leaning toward him. "There's this little girl called Jennifer Strange and her auntie's the bullying sort. Furious with her because no one's dancing with her. So why don't you. I mean, dance with her instead of me. Get it?"

"I would much rather dance with you," said his lordship, feeling somewhat piqued. Never in his well-bred life had any woman suggested that he should spend his time with anyone else.

He leaned back in his chair and drew patterns on the damask tablecloth with his knife. Molly watched his tanned face above his shirt-front. His face was unreadable.

"You must do me one favor in return," he said at last.

"Surely," cried Molly.

"You must promise to drive out with me to-morrow."

Molly bit her lip. She did not really want to be alone with this disturbing man.

"I-I can't," she said. "Lady Fanny says I am not to go out with a man, unchaperoned."

"She'll let you go with me," he said confidently. "After I've had a little talk with her."

"You're very sure of yourself."

"Quite."

"Oh, okay," said Molly while he watched her dismal face with wry amusement.

"Cheer up, dear girl," said Lord David. "It's not a visit to the dentist, you know. Now lead me to your wallflower."

Molly had at least the pleasure of watching Jennifer's face light up as Lord David bowed to her. She found a chance to speak to Jennifer before the ball ended. "There you are," said Molly. "He noticed you after all."

"No thanks to you," said Jennifer triumphantly, looking at Molly out of the corners of her eyes. "I did it all myself."

Molly felt all the rage one usually feels when a doormat type of person gets uppity. Harsh and bitter words rose to her lips. Several choice phrases nearly escaped her. She resolutely choked them all back, except one. "Well," said Molly Maguire, "you can't win 'em all," and walked off primly on her little French heels and left Jennifer to stare after her in surprise.

CHAPTER SIX

Roddy, Marquess of Leamouth, awoke with a groan. Someone was roughly shaking him by the shoulder. What uncouth servants Lord David must have.

"Leave the tea on the table and get out," he moaned without opening his eyes.

"Wake up, you ass!" snapped the well-remembered tones of his host. "How can I plan a campaign with you lying there, snoring your head off?"

Roddy reluctantly opened his eyes. "What's the time?"

"Eight in the morning."

"Eight in the—I say it's a bit much," said Roddy, propping himself up against the pillows. "What do you mean by waking me at dawn?"

"Are you awake now?" demanded David. "Then listen. I blackmail the Maguire girl into driving out with me today and I go to ask Lady Fanny's permission because I don't want a chaperon. All is set. She smiles on me. Later she strides over to me as if she's on the parade ground, fluttering like an effeminate sergeant major, if there is such a thing, and informs me that *you* are hell-bent on joining the expedition and are escorting Mary. How am I to murmur sweet nothings into her shell-like ear with you listening to every word?"

"I won't be listening to every word," Roddy pointed out, "for the simple reason that I hope to be muttering some sweet nothings into a shell-like ear myself. It'll set the atmosphere for you, old man."

"You may have something there," said Lord David thoughtfully. "But I must confess to feeling a little nervous. She's one of those strong, clear-eyed sort of girls who doesn't seem to have any weaknesses. Do you think Miss Molly Maguire has a weakness?"

Fully awake now, the marquess bent his mind to the problem. "I've got an aunt who's as tough as old boots but she loves romances. You know, sort of drivel women read. Find out what Miss Molly reads. Is there a library here?"

"Only one is in the post office. We'll go down there this morning and ask Mrs. Pomfret what Miss Molly reads. Then we'll bone up on it and find what sets her hormones dancing."

Lord David had expected to have to approach the question of what Miss Maguire read in a roundabout sort of way but the postmistress was only too anxious to talk at length about her heroine. "She's so brave and so beautiful," said the elderly postmistress, clasping her hands to her thin bosom. "Just like someone in a book."

"What books does Miss Maguire like to read?" asked Lord David.

"Miss Maguire has just finished this one," said Mrs. Pomfret, picking a book from one of the shelves. "She told me she thought it was wonderful." In her innocence Mrs. Pomfret did not realize that Molly had said the book was wonderful simply because Mrs. Pomfret had obviously thought so herself.

Lord David and the marquess gloomily surveyed the book. It was entitled *The Highland Heart* and showed a red-haired girl in a droopy sort of tea gown sawing away at a violin, against a background of hills and heather. A brooding sort of cove in a kilt was standing down left, staring at this girl with a sort of

"Awakened Conscience" expression, all the while clutching an extremely chic blonde in his arms.

"May I take it?" said Lord David. He was obscurely disappointed in Molly.

"Oh, my lord, *of course*," breathed Mrs. Pomfret, scenting a romance.

Lord David and the marquess walked in silence down to the little harbor of Hadsea. It was a beautiful morning with a fresh breeze scudding across the bay.

"Here, you have a look at it first," said Lord David, handing Roddy the book. "I only need to know the passionate bits. Spare me the rest."

"Right-ho!" said Roddy and bent his fair head over the pages of *The Highland Heart*.

He read and skimmed and read and skimmed and then read and read. "Stop it," said Lord David. "You're not supposed to be enjoying it."

"But it's great stuff," protested his friend. "Oh, well, I'll give you the gist of it.

"There's this laird called Angus who lives up somewhere in the Highlands and runs about the heather with his childhood sweetheart, Morag. Then he goes off to the fleshpots of London, after giving a final ruffle to Morag's hair—"

"That won't get me far," Lord David put in gloomily.

"Don't interrupt. The laird hasn't got warmed up yet."

"Why do lairds go to London?"

"I don't know. To sell grouse or something. Anyway, this Morag scrapes away at her violin in the manse—she's the minister's daughter—and pines for Angus. Angus returns, but on his arm—oh horrors!—is his sinister, overly sophisticated, painted fiancée, Cynthia. Hey, that's a coincidence."

"My Cynthia is not overpainted. Stop digressing," said Lord David.

"Oh, yes, where was I? Well, this Cynthia puts old Morag's eye out, her with painted nails and Paris gowns—Cynthia, I mean. But the veil is torn from Angus's eyes—"

"The veil? What's the chappie wearing a veil for? Is he a pansy?"

"Of course not. That's poetic, that is. And how is the veil torn? Angus comes upon Cynthia beating a kitchen maid with a riding crop. 'Awa, wi' ye,' he cries to the fair Cynthia. 'The veil has been tore frae ma eyes.' See?"

"And Morag throws away her violin and rushes into his arms, I suppose," yawned Lord David.

"Not a bit of it. She's a strong lass, is Morag. 'Ye cannae get roond me, ye wi' yer seductive London ways,' she says, throwing her head back and staring him straight in the eyes. Morag does a lot of that, by the way. Angus strides about the heather in agonies. He remembers all sorts of endearing things about his Morag. How they ran about the braes together and all that. Oh, and he remembers her tending the broken wing of a sick grouse."

"Oh, for Heaven's sake," howled Lord David. "Any decent Highland lass knows exactly what to do with a grouse with a broken wing: wring its neck and pop it in the pot."

"You have no heart," said Roddy severely. "How are you going to charm Miss Molly if you won't listen? Now all seems hopeless for the laird, but the fair Morag has a dog called Hamish—"

"Dear God."

"—called Hamish," repeated Roddy firmly. "Well, this lovable mutt falls in the River Door, which is in spate. The one thing the redoubtable Morag cannot do is swim. She watches in horror as her mutt is swept downstream. But picking up his kilts—what do lairds wear under their kilts?"

"Nothing."

"Filthy beast! Anyway, Angus plunges in at great risk to life and limb and rescues Hamish. He walks toward her, clasping the dripping-wet dog in his arms. 'Oh, Angus,' says Morag. 'Och, Morag,' says he, and clasps her in his strong arms and presses her dear, curly head against his manly bosom."

"How the bloody hell can he clasp Morag with a great wet mutt between them? What happened to the dog?" asked Lord David testily.

Roddy scanned a few pages with a puzzled eye. "That's funny. This writer can't be a dog lover. He presses his firm masculine lips against her soft yielding ones and . . . curtain. That's it."

"But doesn't he ever—"

"No, he doesn't. Just kisses her—and after all that!"

"Here, give me that book," said Lord David suddenly. "Now let me see . . ."

He read for some time. Roddy watched him with amusement, wishing he had brought a camera. The sight of Lord David Manley poring intently over *The Highland Heart* was a sight worth seeing.

"I've got it!" said Lord David at length. "There's a lot of crushing to bosoms goes on in this. Strong, silent stuff. That's obviously what appeals to Miss Maguire. You must lure Mary away somewhere this afternoon and leave me alone with Miss Molly to do some strong, silent crushing."

"Right-ho," said Roddy amiably. "But don't be surprised if she slaps your face!"

* * *

Lord David Manley was brooding exactly like Angus. The foursome of himself and Roddy and the sisters Maguire were seated in a perfect sylvan setting. The sun slanted through a stand of tall, slim birch trees, the river tumbled and sparkled between large boulders. Shy clumps of speedwells and ragged robins peeped out from the shady undergrowth. Bees hummed around the white bramble flowers and birds sang merrily overhead. There was nothing to do on this lazy afternoon but sit and watch the servants unpacking the picnic things.

The servants!

Lord David Manley had not counted on those. Flushed with the triumph of having both protégées escorted by two of England's most eligible bachelors, Lady Fanny had decided that they must have a picnic. The girls could not possibly sit on the grass in their new gowns. Table and chairs must be provided. And so the charming little open carriage bearing the happy foursome had been followed by two carriages of footmen with all the necessary accessories.

The only strong, silent crushing going on was made by the army of footmen as they moved around the small sylvan glade, breathing heavily through their noses, and trying hard, without much success, not to bump into each other.

"Why don't you all go and take a walk somewhere?" David heard Roddy saying to the head footman. "Come back in a couple of hours." Several coins changed hands. The head footman gave a satisfied smirk and soon the carriages bearing the servants could be heard creaking off at a comfortable distance.

Lord David poured out the wine thoughtfully provided by Lady Fanny and set himself to please. Both American girls, he realized with amusement, had easily adopted the speech and manners of their English counterparts. But there was something about them that was still undoubtedly American, apart from the younger one's slight lapses in grammar. He decided it was their open friendliness. There was also a freshness about them and an almost seductive smell of lavender soap and clean linen. He realized with a little shock that some of the debutantes of his acquaintance were not as clean as they might be.

Mary was flirting prettily with Roddy, but Molly seemed unable to relax. Lord David noticed that she kept watching her sister with a little worried expression behind her eyes.

He decided that the time for the strong, silent treatment had arrived. "Miss Molly," he leaned forward. "There is a very pretty path along by the river. Would you care to see it?"

"Oh, yes," said Molly with depressing enthusiasm, "let's all go!"

"Oh, you two go on," said Roddy languidly. "Miss Mary and I will sit here and admire your energy."

After a slight hesitation Molly allowed herself to be led away.

"What a strong character your sister appears to have," said Roddy idly, his long fingers playing with the stem of his wineglass. "But I suppose she's really very romantic."

"I suppose so," said Mary doubtfully.

"You don't seem too sure," teased Roddy. "I'm quite certain that your sister would really fall for the strong, silent, masterful type of man."

"Oh, I shouldn't think so," said Mary. "I guess Molly will always want to help lame ducks. A strong, masterful man would probably just seem like a bully to her, I reckon."

"What about *The Highland Heart*," demanded Roddy. "Mrs. Pomfret assured me that Miss Molly adored it. Had a look at it, you know. Well, the chappie in the book, Angus, you know, seemed to spend his time either brooding or crushing young ladies to his bosom."

"Wasn't it *awful*," said Mary, failing to note the slightly stricken look on the face of her companion. "Of course Molly did not want to hurt Mrs. Pomfret's feelings so she told her it was marvelous. But how we laughed at that terrible book. She said that Angus obviously had something up with his liver and that if she ever met a man like that, she would be tempted to punch him on the nose."

Roddy stirred restlessly on his seat. They were, of course, correctly seated at a picnic table. Lady Fanny had recently seen the famous painting of *Un Déjeuner sur l'Herbe* and had since considered picnicking on the grass the next thing to immorality.

Roddy got to his feet. "Come along, Miss Mary. A walk by the river is just what we need to wake us up after lunch."

Mary was disappointed. This handsome marquess had, until a few minutes ago, seemed perfectly happy to have her all to himself. But she docilely tripped along beside him, trying to match her small steps to his great strides. It was not so much a stroll beside the river, she decided, as a race.

Roddy hoped fervently that Lord David had not gone in for any strong, silent crushing.

Lord David had not yet made any move but was about to do so despite the so far tepid response from his companion. The narrow path had become tortuous and rocky, and there were excellent opportunities for helping her over small obstacles with a strong hand. Molly had looked at him crossly several times and had said something like, "I can manage by myself," but with the noise of the rushing stream he couldn't be sure. There was a large boulder blocking the path. "I had better lift you over that," murmured Lord David seductively.

"What did you say?" demanded Molly.

"I said I'd better help you over that," roared Lord David, beginning to feel like a fool.

"I am perfectly able to manage myself," said Molly for the umpteenth time. "Anyway, I think we had better be getting back."

But Lord David decided to take the plunge. Women usually melted in his arms, didn't they? He was reaching out to grasp Molly by the waist when he heard his name being called.

He swung around, cursing under his breath. Roddy and Mary were hastening up to them, and Roddy's large eyes were signaling warnings for all they were worth.

"I wouldn't exert yourself, David," yelled Roddy. "Remember your condition."

"My condition," repeated his lordship stupidly.

"Yes," roared Roddy, above the noise of the rushing water. "After all, you have got tuberculosis."

"But I thought he was cured," said Molly, staring in amazement at the healthy, tanned face of Lord David.

"Not a bit of it," said Roddy. "Doctors say he could pop off anytime."

Lord David was about to howl that he was perfectly fit when he saw that Molly was looking up at him with a glowing, tender expression.

"We had better go back," said Molly, this time taking Lord David's arm in a comforting clasp. Lord David shut his mouth and allowed Molly to lead him slowly back along the path. At the picnic table she fussed over him like a mother hen, her beautiful eyes wide with sympathy. It was all very pleasant.

He felt a bit of a cad, but Molly's sympathy for the dying man had brought out her feminine side. She had never looked more beautiful. Every line of her strong young body seemed to have grown soft and seductive. As she bent solicitously over him, pouring him a glass of wine, Lord David stared in fascination at her rounded bosom and thought how splendid it would be to put his head down on it and sleep, and hear that gentle American voice cooing in his ears.

On the road home Molly sat very close to him in the carriage. Little black curls escaped from under her frivolous hat. Her mouth was soft and her eyes wide. Lord David was conscious of a heady, exciting sensation. He could feel the response of her body to his, and although they did not even hold hands, he knew that they were making love.

When they reached the Holden home, Lord David sprang out of the carriage, despite Molly's protests, and helped her down. He bent his head and kissed her gloved hand and then looked deep into her beautiful blue eyes. For a long moment, a strong thread of emotion seemed to join them and Lord David realized with a start that for the first time in his life, his heart was in danger. Reluctantly he released her hand and stood watching her while she walked into the house.

Jennifer Strange prized herself out of the shrubbery, her little freckled face screwed up in a rather nasty way. Molly Maguire was a beast! What right had this *foreigner* to go out driving with Lord David when she, Jennifer, had already told Molly her heart's desire. Molly must be punished. Lord David must be punished, and Jennifer Strange would see to that! She tripped demurely home to write a letter to Lord David's fiancée, Lady Cynthia Whitworth.

"Well, well, well," Lord David was saying. "What was all that about?"

Roddy told him. "Mary told me that she only likes lame ducks so it seemed like a stroke of genius. Did you see how she looked at you when she thought you were a dying man?"

"Yes," said Lord David, frowning. "And what is Miss Maguire going to do when she finds out we have tricked her?"

"Oh, she won't," said Roddy blithely. "We'll just change the date of your recovery. But what about Cynthia? She knows you're cured, doesn't she? She'll expect you to make the engagement official."

"That won't be for some time," said Lord David, after some thought. "Cynthia never rushes into anything."

"Well, be careful and don't queer my pitch. I'm getting very fond of Mary. In fact," said Roddy suddenly, "I think I'm in love with her."

Lord David laughed indulgently. "When weren't you in love, Roddy, my boy? You fall in love the way other people catch colds."

"I think I'm serious this time," said Roddy. "Lady Fanny is giving this ball for the girls. You know what? Think I'll pop the question."

"I'll believe that when it happens," said his friend cynically. "Don't spring any surprises on me. Remember, I'm a dying man!"

Lady Cynthia Whitworth slowly put down the letter from Jennifer Strange and touched the bell at her side. "Ah, Bland," she said when her butler answered the summons. "Do we know where to find a detective?"

The butler thought for a minute. "I think, my lady, that there was a certain person who was called in privately to solve the mystery of the Duchess of Earlston's diamonds."

"Oh, that one. Yes. Turned out her son had pinched them. Well, get on to him and ask him to find out all he can about a couple of American heiresses called Molly and Mary Maguire. And tell him I need the information urgently. . . ."

Lady Fanny put down her coffee cup so that it rattled in the saucer. "Oh, dear," she said faintly. "Toby, do listen."

Lord Toby looked at her rather wearily, wondering which facet of his life was about to be disciplined.

"I've a letter here from Lady Cynthia Whitworth. Remember there were rumors that she was to marry Lord David, and then it all petered out?"

"No," said Toby, picking up the morning paper.

"Put that rag down," snapped his wife in her best parade-ground voice. "Pay attention! Lady Cynthia now more or less says that the engagement is still on and that she is coming *here* for the gels' ball. Oh, dear! And I shall have to invite her to the dinner beforehand.

And Molly *has* been making sheep's eyes at Lord David. I don't know what has got into her. She seemed to be *such* a sensible girl. And what does Lord David mean, pray, if his intentions are not honorable?"

"Don't know," muttered her spouse in a voice that clearly meant "Don't care."

"Toby! Come to attention! You are to go 'round there this morning and ask Lord David what he thinks he's playing at."

But for once her husband stood firm. "No, I won't. He's done nothing wrong. He hasn't *courted* Molly. Only taken her out driving now and then. Not the thing at all, Fanny," he added severely. "You should know better."

"I suppose you're right," conceded Lady Fanny sulkily and then said, "I've got it!"

"Got what?"

"Giles."

"Giles? Your nephew? That's the last person we need," said Lord Toby, stirred into rare animation. "Sent down from Oxford because of some barmaid. Tomcat around the casinos. What on earth has got into you, Fanny?"

"I'm sure he has reformed," said Lady Fanny in a grim voice that clearly meant that if he hadn't, he was going to. "And don't you see, he is very attractive. I'll get him here for the night of the ball and get him to pay court to

Molly. That way she won't have time to notice David's engagement."

Lord Toby gave up. Life had a way of coming between him and the sports pages of his morning paper. He was fond of Molly, but the report of yesterday's racing at Sandown came first.

"Do what you want," he said. Dammit, if there hadn't been a horse called Broken Heart—a rank outsider that had galloped home—Now, if he had put a fiver on that, he could have won. . . . He lost himself in pleasant meditation, unaware that his wife had left the room.

CHAPTER SEVEN

Lord David Manley and the Marquess of Leamouth were getting ready for the ball. Both men had also been invited to the preball dinner. "Do you think," said Lord David, wrestling with a recalcitrant collar stud, "that the ladies realize what we have to go through? Do they for one minute consider the hell and discomfort of a collar stud?"

"Shouldn't think so," said Roddy, lounging elegantly in a chair. As usual, his evening clothes looked as if they had been molded to his form. "Think of what the girls have to go through themselves, what with stays and all that."

Lord David suddenly thought of Molly and

undergarments, and the thought seemed to be doing something to his breath. "I hope I don't have to go around punching anyone in the head tonight," he said. "How did you manage with young Bingham, by the way?"

"I did what you told me," said his friend simply. "I appealed to his better nature."

"Well, I couldn't appeal to Cuthbert's better nature," said Lord David, pulling on his white gloves. "He hasn't got one. Don't worry. That was a master stroke of yours . . . about me having tuberculosis, I mean. I don't anticipate any difficulties this evening."

But as he and Roddy walked up the long drive toward the Holden mansion, he was once more aware of that feeling of heady excitement. What would she be wearing? Would she look at him *so*? Feathery pink clouds were spread across the heavens, and the formal gardens of Lady Fanny's estate blazed with color behind their rigid borders of shells.

The band could be heard rehearsing in the ballroom. There came the sweet, lilting strains of a waltz, and Lord David's nostrils were filled with all the evening scents of the garden mixed with the exotic smells of French cooking from the kitchen: wine and roses, sweet-smelling stock and garlic, herbs and dew-laden grass, and damp leaves. Lord David experienced a sudden feeling of tremulous anticipation. He

110

wanted suddenly to stay where he was, in the driveway, experiencing this novel feeling, being aware of every scent and sound of the summer's evening. "I never realized before," he said quietly, "that England was so beautiful."

With strange reluctance he followed Roddy into the house. And there she was. He reflected briefly that Lady Fanny was a genius when it came to choosing clothes for the Maguire sisters. Instead of dressing Molly in debutante white, Lady Fanny had chosen a dress for her in deepest crimson chiffon. It was cut low at the bosom, emphasizing the whiteness of her neck and shoulders. It was swept up at the back into a saucy sort of bustle reminiscent of the 1870s, and her glossy curls were dressed high on her head without any of the fashionable frizzing to spoil them. One deep-scarlet rose was placed behind her ear. Her eyes were like sapphires and just, he noticed with a start, as hard.

A devastatingly good-looking young man appeared at her elbow and led her away. He was about to follow when a well-remembered voice said, "Darling!"

One little word and the enchantment fled, leaving him standing in an overfurnished house, wondering how soon he could escape.

He turned around, and Lady Cynthia Whitworth stood smiling into his eyes. She was nearly as tall as he and built on Junoesque lines. Her blonde hair was worn fashionably low on her brow, her skin was like an enameled rose leaf, and her gown screamed Paris with every stitch. She was all his—and he was suddenly miserable.

He became aware that she was speaking. He had forgotten how ugly her voice was. She had a high, affected drawl.

"Glad to see you back from the land of the dead, darling," she was saying. "I sent the notice of our engagement to the papers. Now, aren't you thrilled?"

"Devastated," he said politely, kissing her porcelain cheek. "There goes the dinner gong."

"You must tell me all about the Maguire sisters," drawled Cynthia as they walked toward the table. "Quite characters, I imagine. Is that them? How very dark, to be sure, but I've heard it said that a lot of those American girls have *Negro* blood in them."

"Nonsense," said his lordship with a cutting edge to his voice. "Whitest skins I've seen in years. Anyway, the latest rage of Paris has Negro blood in her. Skin like honey. All the fellows are mad about her."

"Dear me," said Lady Cynthia, raising her penciled eyebrows. "How democratic you have become. It must be the American influence."

Roddy moved behind Lord David to find his own seat. "Her with her painted nails and Paris gowns," he murmured in Lord David's ear. Lord David let out a sudden unmanly giggle and Cynthia looked at him with narrowed eyes and then focussed her attention on Molly, who was seated across the table from her, next to Giles.

"You won't object to me speaking across the table, will you, Miss Maguire?" she said sweetly. "My fiancé informs me that you Americans do not believe in our stuffy English conventions."

The word "fiancé" pierced Molly's heart like a knife but no trace of what she felt showed on her face.

"You make me nervous," said Molly equally sweetly. "You see, Lady Cynthia, I have learned that in English society, if anyone begins by referring to the free and easy ways of the Americans, it usually means they are about to take some terrible liberty."

Lady Cynthia's mouth curled up in a thin line. *That explains the mystery of the Mona Lisa,* thought Molly suddenly. *Leonardo da Vinci had probably just fallen on his palette knife or tripped over his easel.*

"But I know a lot about you, you see," said Lady Cynthia. "And I do admire you so— working away like slaves in that little shop in

Brooklyn. And to make your family fortunes by inventing a cough syrup with that hilarious name 'Maguires' Leprechaun Dew.'" She gave the sort of laugh that is usually described as tinkling.

From the head of the table Lady Fanny emitted a low groan.

"I say," said Giles suddenly. "Did you really? By Jove, I think that's marvelous. Takes brains and guts. Tell us about it."

And to Lady Cynthia's chagrin that is exactly what Molly did. She mimicked the accents of Dolores and Jimmy perfectly. The whole table rocked with appreciative laughter. How English society loves a character, and if that character is very rich and very beautiful, then near adoration sets in.

Lady Cynthia realized bitterly that instead of ruining the Maguire sisters as she had, of course, planned, she had set their little footsteps well on the path to the most successful London Season two young ladies were ever likely to experience.

Lord David watched Molly's usually mobile face for some signs of shock or hurt at the news that he was engaged. But Giles's handsome head was bent over her in an irritatingly possessive way and Molly was laughing appreciatively at something he was saying.

At least Cynthia had done her no social

damage. He found himself wanting to explain something about his relationship with Cynthia to Molly, but the conventions forbade it and he did not quite realize why he wanted to do any explaining anyway.

Suddenly Cynthia gave that terrible little tinkling laugh and raised her glass. "I think we should all drink a toast," she said, "to David's complete recovery."

Molly's face showed nothing but genuine delight. "When did you get the news?" she cried. Mary was smiling at him as well and something seemed to have happened to his voice.

"Oh, David knew *ages* ago, didn't you, darling?" said Cynthia.

Why couldn't he say anything? For one second both the Maguire sisters were expressionless as if they had been wiped with a sponge. Then Molly turned and began to chatter to Giles, and Mary turned her shoulder on Roddy and gave her full attention to her other neighbor.

What a bloody rotten country England was, reflected Lord David. He knew instinctively that the Maguire sisters would never forgive the deceit unless he did something very dramatic. Soon the ballroom stretched before him like a piece of polished eternity. Cynthia was always at his side, one gloved hand securely grasping his arm, basking in compliments on her beauty and congratulations on her engagement. And Molly was dancing and dancing with Giles, always on some other part of the floor.

He finally escaped into the garden and communed moodily with the night flowers. He heard the murmur of voices behind a low hedge and was about to retreat. He was then stopped in his tracks by the unmistakable sound of Roddy's voice: "Oh, Mary! I am most awfully in love with you."

"Oh, yeah?" said the unmistakable voice of Miss Mary Maguire. "Well, now you've said your party piece, can we go back in?"

"But Mary! I'm asking you to marry me."

"No, you're not," came Mary's transatlantic twang, very pronounced. "You're playing at proposing to me in the way that that friend of yours pretended to be a dying man to trick my sister. Bet you both had a good laugh about it."

"But we didn't—"

There was the quick swish of a dress. Lord David tried to retreat but it was too late. In the pale light of the moon, he could see Mary's eyes glistening with contempt.

"Eavesdropping, my lord?" she said coldly. He put out a restraining arm only to find that Mary had whisked off and that he was clutching Roddy.

Both friends glared at each other. Both said in unison, "It's all your fault."

"We won't get very far by quarreling," said Lord David. "We're really making asses of ourselves over a couple of quite ordinary girls. Come, now, Roddy! How many times have you been in love before and got over it?"

"It was never like this before," said Roddy, shaking his head.

"Yes, it was, because that is exactly what you say each time," said Lord David. "The Maguire sisters are, after all, just like any other girls. Well . . . they are . . . aren't they . . . ?"

Mary went in search of her sister and eventually found her standing in the shadow of the curtains at one of the long windows overlooking the garden. Her large eyes were bright with unshed tears. Mary put an arm around her waist and both girls stood silently, listening to the music and watching the moving patterns of the leaves on the moonlit lawns.

"They're all so cruel," said Molly in a hard, flat voice. "I wish we were back in Brooklyn."

"We'll leave then," said Mary eagerly. "Right now."

Molly looked at her sadly. "That's just what I want to do. But I can't. I'm stubborn and I'm human enough to want revenge. Lord

David Manley is going to wish that he never set eyes on me by the time I'm finished with him."

"Oh, well," sighed Mary. "I'll stick it out. I've just refused the marquess, so that's a bit of revenge."

"Why?" asked Molly. "I thought you were sweet on him."

Mary wrinkled her brow. "I dunno," she said at last. "I felt he was playing a game just like Lord David. I thought that by the morning he would be laughing and saying he had never said a word." She turned her face away to hide the look of hurt in her large eyes from her sister.

"You did the right thing, Mary," said Molly, giving her a hug. "Some of them here can be pretty nasty about Americans. One woman asked me my *real* Christian name and I said, 'Molly.' 'Oh, that's a *nickname*,' she giggled. 'You Americans are so *weird*. Frightfully so, don't you think? There was a chappie from New York called Harry and he had been christened Harry. He didn't even know his real name was Henry.' 'So what?' I asked. 'I can see it is of not the slightest use trying to talk to you,' she said, giggling. 'You speak a different language. My God, the French are easier to understand.' Then she told me that Molly

118

was only a nickname for Mary and that we were *both* called Mary."

"Well, no one in New York would understand *them*," said Mary warmly. "Have you heard the latest baby talk? 'Is oo having a deevie time?' Pah!"

"Anyway," said Molly. "I'm so glad you turned down the marquess. I think he was acting all along, Mary. I'm downright proud of you for being so sensible. Now, why are we looking so dismal?" Her voice changed to its new English accent.

"After all, what a frightfully jolly, ripping evening!"

"Quite," said Mary, and then both girls giggled despite their hurt.

Molly wound her arm around her sister's waist. "Onward, Miss Mary Maguire! Let's go back in there and knock 'em in the aisles!"

Heads high, fans waving, skirts swinging, the Maguire sisters returned to the ballroom and broke more hearts that evening than they were ever likely to know.

Lady Cynthia swung around in Lord David's arms and watched the sisters' success from under her eyelashes. They had no *right* to be so successful. Little upstarts! What had happened to the English aristocracy? Lady Cynthia had tried to drop a word in Lady Fanny's ear but Lady Fanny had refused to listen. "Vulgar manners? Nonsense!" she said roundly. "The little one's grammar was a teensy bit strange at first, I'll admit. But they are both kind-hearted gels with a great deal of charm. And so disciplined! They are always so fresh and clean and energetic. And lots of Americans come from good British stock."

"Not the Maguire sisters," Lady Cynthia had acidly pointed out. "Their father is Irish and the mother is Polish."

Lady Fanny had surveyed Lady Cynthia with an uncomfortably shrewd look in her pale eyes. "How well informed you are, my dear," she had said sweetly. "I didn't even know that and I have met both parents, but then I didn't think it *important* enough to find out."

Lady Cynthia had been obliged to spend quite some time smoothing down Lady Fanny's ruffled feathers. After all, she, Cynthia, wished to stay on as a house guest. She had expected Lord David to return with her to London in the morning, but that infuriating man had said that the air of Hadsea was good for him and showed every intention of spending several more weeks in this provincial backwater. Certainly Lord David had been flatteringly attentive and had held her very close indeed every time he danced past Molly Maguire.

Somehow, somewhere, decided Cynthia, she must take the limelight away from the Maguires, even if it meant suffering the life of this poky little town. She would wait and watch and snatch at any opportunity that presented itself.

CHAPTER EIGHT

"Where are the girls?" demanded Lady Cynthia languidly. Several uneventful days had passed since the ball, and Molly and Mary appeared to be absent most of the time.

"On their bicycles," said Lady Fanny, looking up from a pile of correspondence.

"*Bicycles*! How very suffragette of them. Are they wearing bloomers?"

"Thank goodness, no!" said Lady Fanny. "I would have refused to let them buy bicycles if they meant to appear like freaks. Molly explained to me that they would wear divided skirts, and I must say she has excellent taste. Very *chic*. Like little sailor outfits, and *really* you could not tell their skirts were divided.

They look just like ordinary walking dresses . . . when they're walking that is—" She broke off to watch with horrified amazement as Cynthia took out a slim gold case, extracted a cigarette, and lit it with a practiced hand.

"*Cynthia!*" shrieked Lady Fanny. "If you must indulge in that filthy habit, I insist you go to the smoking room *immediately*. Oh, dear, Wembley, what is it now?"

"Mrs. Pomfret from the post office, my lady," said the butler.

"What on earth does she want?" said Lady Fanny crossly. "Why isn't she post-officing or something?"

"She wished to see Miss Maguire," said Wembley. "I informed her that the Misses Maguire were bicycling, and she begged to have a word with you, my lady."

"I haven't got the time. Molly does make such odd friends. First Mrs. Pomfret and then two grubby children calling with bunches of flowers . . ."

"I'll see her," said Lady Cynthia. The more she could find out about Molly the better. "Show her into the smoking room, Wembley."

To Lady Cynthia's irritation, Wembley waited for his mistress's orders. "Very well," said Lady Fanny grumpily. "Grateful to you, Cynthia. But be nice to her, mind."

"Of course," drawled Cynthia, moving to the door. "I always am."

Mrs. Pomfret nervously eyed the beauty in front of her and tried not to look too shocked at the cigarette. It was not for her to question the ways of her betters. She plunged into speech.

"I am sorry to take up your time, Lady Cynthia," she said timidly. "Perhaps you may be able to advise me. I have written a little play for our local pageant and I wish Miss Molly to play the part of Queen Winifred."

"Who on earth is Queen Winifred?" drawled Cynthia, flicking ash on the carpet.

Mrs. Pomfret blushed painfully. The weather was extremely hot and she had not been able to afford to cater for this strangely warm English summer by buying a suitable dress. She was aware of her dowdy, well-worn tweeds and of the little cracks and holes in her straw hat, which her sensitive nature was sure that Lady Cynthia had noticed despite the fact that she had tried to refurbish it by winding her best silk scarf around the crown.

"Queen Winifred is my invention, my lady. I write the plays each year for the pageant but *this* year I wrote the main part especially for Miss Maguire. She is so brave and beautiful . . ." Mrs. Pomfret's voice trailed away miserably under the ice of Lady Cynthia's gaze.

"And who else takes part in this little pageant?" inquired Cynthia.

"Everyone . . . everyone in the town, that is," said Mrs. Pomfret, forgetting her nervousness in sudden enthusiasm for her pet subject. *This* year it is to be a Norman invasion, and Queen Winifred is a Saxon queen. It all takes place in the harbor and some of the townspeople play the parts of the invading Normans—the fishermen kindly lend their boats—and the other townspeople play the besieged Saxons."

"But what does Queen Winifred *do?*"

"Well, after the Norman soldiers land, they are led by Baron Guy de Boissy. The queen rides toward him and says, 'Forsooth, sirrah, begone from this noble city.'

"'*Merde* to that,' he roars . . . that's French, you know."

"I know," said Cynthia sweetly. "Do you know what it means?"

"Something French anyway," said Mrs. Pomfret bravely.

Cynthia told her what it meant.

Mrs. Pomfret's mouth fell open in dismay but she rallied quickly. "Then he shall say 'zounds' or something. Then he is struck by Winifred's beauty. 'If you come to France with me, fair maiden,' he says, 'I wilt not attack thy town.'

" 'I wilt,' says the queen. They set sail after the townspeople have cheered Winifred to the echo, throwing roses under the hoofs of her white palfrey."

Cynthia narrowed her eyes. It was all silly, childish nonsense, she knew. But she could see herself on a white horse with the cheering crowds around her. She could imagine David looking at her with admiration and the Maguire sisters being forced to play the part of Saxon peasants. She would insist that they darkened their skins with burnt cork.

"Now, Mrs. Pomfret," she said, bestowing a glittering smile on the postmistress. "Only consider. A Saxon queen should be fair. Molly is dark. But I will save the day for you. Now, I know I am going to amaze you, but *I* shall play the part of Queen Winifred. Now, not another word. I do not want to be embarrassed by gratitude. Lord David will play the Norman king, of course . . . or leader."

Mrs. Pomfret summoned up her small stock of courage. "But I-I h-had set my h-heart on Miss Maguire," she stammered.

"You are ungrateful," said Cynthia with a steely note in her voice. "Molly is American, and you cannot have an American as a Saxon queen."

Mrs. Pomfret shook her head dumbly. Her

courage had fled. She only hoped Molly would understand.

Molly was very sympathetic. She sat in the dark kitchen of the post office later that day with Mary and Mrs. Pomfret. The girls' bicycles were propped around the back of the shop to escape the eagle eyes of Giles. Molly had found that young man's attentions unwelcome and boring. It was bad enough to have him always present at the house, without having him spoiling their cycling tours.

"Let Cynthia take the part," said Molly. "She *is* very beautiful. Mary and I will watch from the sidelines. I must say I am surprised Lord David is going to take part. I thought he would be too grand for the town pageant."

"Oh, he *is*," said Mrs. Pomfret. "He told me he wanted to have nothing to do with it, so the main male part is to be taken by the mayor, Mister Henderson, as usual."

"Cynthia won't like that," said Molly thoughtfully. Mr. Henderson was pompous, fat, and florid. The idea of him bearing Cynthia off to France suddenly made her giggle.

"When is this all to take place?" she asked.

"Next week—on Saturday," said Mrs. Pomfret, putting a plate of hot buttered crumpets on the table. "We never have much rehearsal because it is always a little bit the same. You know, an invasion and so on. Last year it was Queen Elizabeth and the Spanish invasion."

"And who took the part of Queen Elizabeth?"

"I did," said Mrs. Pomfret, flushing slightly. "It was the most marvelous moment of my life. But you see I couldn't this year because I wrote about a *young* queen and I did so want it to be you."

"Don't worry," said Molly gently, "I couldn't have taken the part. I can't ride a horse, and you couldn't have Queen Winifred riding down to the waterfront on a bicycle."

"I don't know," said Mrs. Pomfret, made stubborn by disappointment. She did not like Lady Cynthia. "A few years ago Mister Henderson insisted on using his new motorcar in the pageant. It was all about Druids—"

"Invading England?"

"Dear me, no! Welcoming the arrival of Christian missionaries in their coracles. Well, we couldn't have a motorcar in that. So modern. But the Boy Scouts covered it with painted canvas and turned the motor into a sacrificial chariot, which really looked splendid, although it did take its victims to the altar rather *fast*. Now then. I hear someone in the shop."

Molly's sharp ears picked up the sound of Lord David's voice. "Let me hear what he's saying," she said, getting to her feet. "Probably planning his funeral."

She crept to the door and opened it a crack. Lord David's strong voice sailed into the room. "I don't think this idea of yours is going to work," they heard him say. "We came a cropper on *The Highland Heart*. This time ask Mrs. Pomfret what Molly reads—what she has chosen *herself*."

"Right-ho!" replied Roddy, giving the bell on the counter a smart ring.

Mrs. Pomfret looked at the girls with bewildered eyes. "I don't understand. Why should they want to know what you read, Molly?"

"Anyway, it can't do any harm to find out what the man of her dreams is like," said Roddy with fatal clarity.

"It's a good thing you didn't go in for any of that strong, silent crushing in *The Highland Heart*," he went on. "I tell you, find out what she reads and you'll find out the kind of man she likes."

Molly's lips folded into a thin line. She looked around the kitchen. A newly opened parcel of books for the library lay on the kitchen table. On the top was one with a brightly colored jacket portraying a Regency buck surveying a simpering miss through his quizzing glass. It was entitled *The Marquess of Maidstone's Downfall*.

"Give this to Lord David," whispered Molly urgently. "Tell him this is my favorite book and I wish I could meet a man like the Marquess of Maidstone."

Mrs. Pomfret looked at Molly in bewilderment but she had done exactly what Molly had wanted before and had thereby rid herself of a blackmailer. With simple trust, the postmistress picked up the book. She was a strictly honest woman but for Molly Maguire she would have lied to the Archangel Gabriel himself. She hurried off into the outer shop.

Molly looked thoughtfully at her sister. "It's a long time since we've been to confession, Mary," she said.

"How can we?" said Mary with a mouthful of cake. "The nearest chapel is miles from here."

"We've got our bicycles."

"So we have," said Mary, brightening. "But we'll be late home for dinner and Lady Fanny will say we are so *undisciplined*."

"We've been very good up till now," said Molly, laughing.

"Man of my dreams, indeed! I wonder why he bothers? Probably he and Cynthia are planning to play some terrible practical joke on me. It's just the sort of thing they would do!"

• • •

Lord David and the marquess climbed to the top of an old ruined tower at the end of the harbor wall and sat down to peruse *The Marquess of Maidstone's Downfall*.

"Are you sure you want to be bothered with this?" said Roddy. "What was all that stuff the night of the ball about the Maguire sisters just being like any other girls?"

"I changed my mind," said Lord David briefly. "Read."

"Oh, very well," said Robby gloomily. "But it looks like the most awful sludge."

He bent his head over the book. Lord David propped his back against the crumbling wall of the tower and surveyed the scenery.

The sun was low in the sky, casting a crimson path across the still water and bathing the old buildings around the harbor in a rosy glow. Swallows darted and skimmed over dark-blue water. People were walking about lazily or talking in groups. One by one the fishing boats were coming home. There was a faint smell of woodsmoke and fish and strong tea mixed with the piny smells of the woods behind the town. It all seemed very peaceful. For the first time he was aware of a feeling of holiday. He thought briefly of Cynthia. How on earth had he ever managed to let himself get embroiled? All he could do was to keep postponing the wedding date until she became tired of him. He had a longing to cycle slowly along the country lanes with Molly Maguire.

Far away along the curve of the beach, the sturdy horses were still pulling the brightly colored bathing machines into the sea, the women screaming with mock fear as they teetered down the wooden steps into the water. He wondered if Molly went bathing and was stirred by the age-old aphrodisiac of the sea, and the thought of Miss Maguire in a bathing dress.

Roddy's voice broke into his thoughts. "This should be easy," said the marquess. "Now this type of hero doesn't go in for any strong, silent clutching. He actually presses her hand fervently at Almack's on page one hundred and two."

"You mean in the gambling club?"

"No, silly. Almack's assembly rooms. Marriage market of Regency days."

"According to my old rip of a grandfather, they got up to a lot more than holding hands, even at Almack's," said Lord David testily, "and what *is* this Marquess of Maidstone's downfall?"

"His downfall," said Roddy, reading quickly, "is a shy country girl who is fresh and natural and not like those other painted hussies. Her name is Belinda and she blushes and faints a lot."

"Forget it," said Lord David. "Molly is not going to faint and blush."

"Don't interrupt," said Roddy. "The marquess is described as having an indolent manner, with indolent eyelids that seem to be closed half the time. Occasionally his eyes glint with mocking laughter as he flicks a speck of dust from the high gloss of his Hessians."

"Sounds like a twit," said Lord David. "How does the fair Belinda react to this half-awake lord?"

"'He smiled down at her from under heavy drooping lids and she trembled with an awakened passion,'" read Roddy. "I'll tell you why the girls like this sort of book and why maybe they don't like us—particularly with them being Americans. We don't behave like aristocrats. That's what! Where is our languid indifference? One minute you're swearing at Molly, the next you're trying to play on her sympathies. As for me, I'm down on my knees in the wet grass asking Mary to marry me. We must be standoffish. Born to command and all that rot."

"But how does this marquess eventually get to first base?—as the Maguires would no doubt say."

"He clasps her firmly and tenderly in his strong arms and kisses her passionately on the mouth. She trembles at his touch and faints from an excess of emotion. That's on the last page."

"She sounds like a bore in bed," said Lord David.

"Tut, tut. They don't get as far as that! Oh, *I* see. He rescues her from a highwayman."

"Well, that's out for a start," said Lord David moodily. "Come along. We're invited to the Holdens for dinner. At least that way we'll get to look at them."

But there was no sign of the Maguire sisters at the dinner table. Cynthia looked particularly glowing and beautiful. Giles was moody and silent—Molly Maguire had paid him no attention at all at the ball and had laughed at all his very best compliments. Lord Toby was staring moodily down at his dish of *Coquilles St. Jacques,* already seeing in his mind's eye the scallop shells being scrubbed and cleaned in the kitchen so that the soulless Scottish gnome gardeners could regiment another flower bed. Roddy was plainly disappointed and showed it. Lady Fanny fretted over the lack of discipline in the young in general and in two American misses in particular, and it was left to Lord David and Cynthia to keep the conversational ball rolling.

Cynthia had been to a dress rehearsal of

the pageant and was being very witty and amusing at the expense of the local yokels. She was indeed very funny and Lord David found to his irritation that he was becoming defensive about the townspeople. He thought the pageant was a splendid idea, and Cynthia should be flattered that she had been chosen to play the leading part.

"But she wasn't," said Giles with happy malice. "Mrs. Pomfret wanted Molly to play the part and Cynthia insisted that she play it herself."

There was a frigid, well-bred silence and then everyone began to talk rapidly about something else.

Course followed course and still the Maguires had not returned. Lord David reflected that under normal circumstances he would have been quite worried about their nonappearance but thought cynically that the girls had heard that he and Roddy were to be dinner guests and had decided to stay away.

Lady Fanny continued to worry. "I really think I must send the servants out to look for them. It is not like the girls to be late, is it Wembley?"

"No, indeed, my lady," said the butler, who had warmed to the Maguire sisters considerably since Lady Cynthia's arrival. "The Misses Maguire, if I may say so, my lady, would *never* be late for dinner. They are too considerate of the servants." Lady Cynthia seemed to have doubled the work of the household with her perpetual inconsiderate demands.

Lord David felt the beginning of a small stab of panic.

"Come along, Roddy," he said with forced cheerfulness, "let's go Maguire hunting." He added under his breath after they had left the dining room, "If they are making fools of us, I'll wring their necks."

The girls were indeed late. They had found a small Roman Catholic chapel several miles from Hadsea. By some strange coincidence, the priest, Father McGarry, was American-Irish. The girls attended the service and stayed to talk to their countryman while the light faded outside and a chill wind corrugated the gray sea.

Molly finally became aware of the time. Both hurriedly made their good-byes, leapt onto their bicycles, and pedaled off furiously along the narrow country lanes. "When we get to the top of this steep hill," said Molly, panting, "we can really race down the other side." Despite her bitterness over the trick he had played on her, she had an urgent longing to see Lord David again. She was also worried about her sister. It was always hard to tell what Mary was thinking. She had been very quiet and withdrawn since the night of the ball. They reached the top of the hill, and the long, narrow chalky road stretched all the way downward. The countryside was deserted apart from the thick-set figure of a man standing in one of the fields.

Molly took a deep breath. "Here we go, Mary!" she called. And pedaling as fast as she could, she took off down the hill, skirts flying, hat tugging against the restraint of the hat guard, sailor collar streaming out behind her, racing down through the dimming evening light. Mary drew along beside her and neck and neck the sisters raced down, faster and faster. They did not see the glittering wire stretched breast-high across the road.

Molly felt a tremendous wrench at her chest. Her bicycle flew out from under her and she sailed dizzily into the air before landing with a sickening crash on the hard pebbles of the road. Mary was lying in the ditch like a broken doll.

"Now iffen I'd 'a put the wire higher, I'd ha' broken yer neck," said a voice above her.

Her eyes blurred with pain, Molly looked up, straight into the grinning face of Mrs. Pomfret's blackmailer, Billy Barnstable.

* * *

"The chapel," said Lord David as he and Roddy rode at a leisurely pace in the direction the girls had first taken. "What on earth do they want to go to church in the middle of the week for? Sundays are enough for me."

"Don't know," said Roddy, "not being a Catholic myself. I believe it takes 'em that way."

Mrs. Pomfret had told their lordships that the girls had planned to attend church. Both men felt that the girls' absence from the dinner table was accounted for and had lost their fears. There was no doubt that it was a lovely evening and that somewhere on the road in front of them were the Maguire sisters. They decided to keep up their search.

"Perhaps they have been held up by a highwayman," teased Roddy. "That way, you will be able to make her faint with passion as you toy with your quizzing glass."

"Don't be filthy," remarked Lord David idly. "I say, that's a big hill up on the other side. What energy! Imagine pedaling a bicycle all the way up that!"

"Look!" said Roddy urgently.

In the dim greenish light at the foot of the hill, the squat figure of a man was aiming blows with a cudgel at a girl who was writhing away from him on the dusty road.

Both men spurred their horses.

Billy Barnstable heard the sound of the galloping hoofs and plunged through the thorn hedge that bordered the road and started to run across the fields. Roddy rushed to where the still body of Mary was lying, but Lord David rode on, trying to find a gap in the hedge so that he could pursue Molly's attacker.

But by the time he finally plunged into the field and rode across it, there was no sign of anyone at all.

When he got back to the scene of the accident, Mary had recovered. Lord David registered with some surprise that Roddy looked almost as white as Mary. Molly was struggling painfully to her feet. Her skirt was torn, her hat was lying in the road, and her hair was escaping from its pins. He stretched out his hands to help her. She tried to avoid him but stumbled and fell into his arms instead. He felt her trembling against him and realized with a queer little wrench of tenderness that she was still afraid. He thought he heard her murmur, "I always hated that fellow," and looked down at her curiously.

"Have you seen your assailant before?" he said in a voice sharpened with anxiety. "You recognized him?"

Molly thought quickly. If she told anyone that she had recognized Billy Barnstable, he would be dragged before the magistrates and she felt sure Billy would broadcast Mrs. Pomfret's pathetic story all over town out of sheer spite.

"No, never. I've never seen him in my life before," she said, throwing a warning look at her sister, who was being held tightly in Roddy's arms. Lord David looked at her curiously but her expression in the dim twilight was unreadable. Molly became aware that he was holding her very closely and tried to extricate herself but she still felt weak and faint and staggered into his arms again. Now was the time to kiss her. But, reflected Lord David, the heroes of Molly's romances did not seem to be hidebound by what was good or bad form and it was definitely "not done" to take advantage of this occasion.

He led her gently over to her sister instead. Mary looked in much worse condition than Molly, as if she might faint again at any minute. Roddy eased her down tenderly onto a hillock of grass beside the road. "I'd better ride to the Holdens for the carriage," he said. "You had better stay with the ladies, David." And with a final, worried look at Mary, he rode off.

Molly and David sat down apart from Mary and conversed in low voices. Molly was anxious to lead the conversation away from the subject of the accident. Lord David sensed this and knew it was not the time to probe any further. He contented himself by asking questions about her life in America and privately thought it sounded very grim and that the Maguire parents were behaving in a stupid and insensitive way. He then took the opportunity to apologize for his lie about his illness. Molly was so grateful to her rescuer that she had already forgiven him. She longed to ask him about his peculiar engagement to Lady Cynthia but realized with a little pang of disappointment that he would not discuss his fiancée.

He began to talk to her of his estates and of the improvements that he hoped to make and Molly, listening to the light, pleasant, drawling voice, found it hard to believe that this was the same man who had shouted so savagely at his servants. She studied his hawklike profile: the peculiarly slanting eyebrows, and the thick black hair. He suddenly turned, his face illuminated by the rising moon, and looked full at her. She felt as if something was happening to her breath. All the sights and sounds of the night seemed immensely clarified: the wind hissing across the field of corn; the rustle of some night creature nearby; the moonlight washing over the fields, highlighting the plains of her companion's face. He leaned slowly toward her, his face very tense. And then the sound of rapidly approaching horses' hoofs broke the spell. Molly blinked as if she had been asleep, and Lord David rose regretfully to his feet. He turned for a second and looked curiously down at his companion.

I'm in love with her, he thought with some surprise. *I'm very much in love and I just don't know what to do.*

There was, indeed, very little he seemed able to do about it in the days before the pageant. Cynthia was fortunately away most of the time, rehearsing her part, but Mary had been kept to her room to recover from her ordeal and Molly spent most of her time abovestairs with her, and the only good thing about that was that Giles had left in disgust. He learned that the sisters planned to attend the pageant but not take part in it; however, they had refused, through the medium of the butler, Wembley, his offer of escort. He had been visited by the local police inspector and had been puzzled by the girls' description of a tall, thin, scarred assailant. He was more than ever convinced that their attacker had been someone they both knew and someone they were shielding from the police.

The day of the pageant dawned warm and fair. People everywhere were talking about this incredible summer and the mayor had posted notices around the town advising the people to ration their use of water. Cynthia had scorned the use of the local dressmaker and had had her costume designed and made in London. Molly and Mary were of the very few not taking active part so they walked slowly down to the harbor—still feeling stiff and sore after their ordeal—to climb to the top of the ruined tower in order to get a good view. The water in the harbor looked like glass, and the fishing boats stood ready for the "invasion," with cardboard shields along their sides and all the fishermen, obviously having a tremendous time, dressed up in armor made from silver paper. The mayor did not look a very convincing Norman baron, for although his armor was real, borrowed from the local museum, he had insisted on retaining his pince-nez, his high celluloid collar, and his necktie.

The townspeople in the harbor front were all turned out in what they fondly considered to be Saxon dress and the children were obviously having a marvelous time. Molly noticed two little boys in Norfolk knickers standing at the edge of the water in front of the crowd. They had, for some reason, not dressed up in costume like the rest of their friends. With a start,

Molly recognized the twins—Bobby and Jim.

The fact was that Bobby and Jim had learned that their heroine was not to take part in the pageant and had therefore consented to wear their Sunday best instead of costumes.

There was a strangled fanfare of trumpets and Cynthia made her entrance. And what an entrance! She had not been popular with the townspeople but every single one gave her a hearty cheer. She looked like a princess out of a fairy tale, her blonde hair hanging to her shoulders in two thick gold braids. A tiny gold crown was perched on her head and she wore a scarlet-and-ermine robe. She was seated on a magnificent white horse, which pranced and curvetted in the best manner. Molly saw Lord David at the edge of the crowd. He was watching Cynthia. She experienced the awful wrenching pangs of jealousy and turned her head away to look anywhere else but at Cynthia.

There were the twins, being pushed precariously near the edge of the harbor by the crowd. Molly watched anxiously. Everyone was trying to get a look at Cynthia, and the cheering and the noise of the trumpets seemed very loud even at the top of the tower.

The crowd swayed and pushed and one of the twins was catapulted into the water.

Molly sprang onto the parapet of the tower,

pushing back Mary's restraining hands. She raised her arms above her head and prepared to dive.

A woman in the crowd saw the poised figure on the tower and screamed and screamed, pointing upward. The trumpets stopped. Everyone looked up. No one had noticed the boy struggling in the water, despite the frantic yells of his twin.

Lord David pushed and pushed, trying to fight his way to the front, trying to call to the figure on the tower not to do it. This had all taken a matter of seconds.

And then Molly Maguire dived. It was madness—it was incredible. She cut the water with hardly a splash and swam in an efficient crawl to where the twin had disappeared. She disappeared under the water again, while the people around the other twin, who turned out to be Bobby, finally managed to tell everyone around him that Jim had fallen in and Miss Maguire had gone to rescue him. The news spread in seconds. There was an agonizing wait and then Molly's head broke the water, pulling the limp body of Jim to the steps cut into the harbor wall. Willing hands helped her out and then watched again in silence as the redoubtable Molly began to pump water out of the boy's lungs. Jim sat up, vomited, and then began to cry in great, healthy, roaring shouts.

His mother, Mrs. Wheelan, struggled to the front of the crowd and flung her arms around the startled and dripping-wet Molly and gave her a resounding kiss.

What a cheer went up as Molly, wet and blushing, made her way through the crowd. The Saxon peasants who had been standing ready to throw rose petals at the feet of Lady Cynthia threw them at Molly instead. Cheer upon cheer rent the summer air and the town band, overcome with emotion, burst into "Rule Britannia!" and everyone joined in and sang until they were hoarse, never stopping to wonder what "Rule Britannia!" had to do with an American miss.

A great bouquet of flowers, intended for presentation to Queen Winifred, was presented to Molly instead.

Cynthia sat as still as a statue on her white horse, ignored by everyone, watching and watching as Molly and her procession neared where Lord David and the marquess were standing.

"Please go and see if you can find Mary," said Molly to Roddy. "She is not very strong yet and I don't want her to be pushed around in the crowd."

Roddy ran off on his errand. Molly paused for a moment, looking up at Lord David. Then, seized by an impulse, she took a white rose from her bouquet and handed it to him. He accepted it gravely. The procession moved on. He stood quite still, looking after her for a long time after she had disappeared from sight.

Lady Cynthia became aware that someone was calling her name. She dragged her eyes away from Lord David and looked down. Cuthbert Postlethwaite was looking up at her. "Been watching the end of your engagement, Cynth?" he drawled. "David seems quite smitten."

"Nonsense," said Cynthia with a light laugh. "David . . . fall for a little upstart with *me* around? You've been drinking."

Cuthbert gave a massive shrug. "Oh, well, if you want to sit on your high horse, in every sense of the word, and not do anything about it when I'm ready and willing to help you get your revenge . . ."

"Here . . . help me down," she said suddenly. "I'm sure you're talking rubbish but I want to get away from the local yokels. Have you got your motorcar? Good. You can drive me somewhere where they serve a really good afternoon tea."

Half an hour later they were cozily ensconced in the parlor of a tea shop in a nearby village. Cynthia looked around disapprovingly at the many brass bowls of flowers, knickknacks, brass ornaments, pictures framed in passe-partout, and an assortment of china gnomes on the mantelshelf.

"What a lot of junk," she said caustically. "Why doesn't the silly woman realize she is simply making work for herself by dusting all that trash?"

"Some people would think it cozy," remarked Cuthbert amiably.

Cynthia wrinkled her pretty nose in disdain. "We didn't come here to discuss the artistic foibles of the village frump," she remarked, indifferent to the fact that the "village frump" was placing the cake stand on the table and could hear every word.

"No," said Cuthbert. "The subject is the Maguire sisters. I want to pay David back. I want to get at him by driving the oldest girl, Molly, back to the States. I've already heard rumors that she doesn't like it here."

"And what is your plan?" asked Cynthia curiously.

"Well, you know that great pile of a place I live in . . . you know, moat, turrets, battlements, the lot . . . ?"

"Yes, yes, yes. What's that to do with it?"

"Give me time to explain. Lady Fanny has always wanted an invitation to my home but I've never asked her because she's a bossy sort of woman. She'd jump at the chance of a visit. I'll invite Fanny and the Maguires *and* Lord

David and Roddy and then I'll set the stage. I'll *haunt* the Maguire sisters."

"Pooh!" said Cynthia, shifting restlessly in her seat. "If they're silly enough to fall for it, David and Roddy will put them wise."

"You must let me explain," said Cuthbert angrily. "Now look here, you don't think I'm going to run along the battlements in a sheet or anything stupid like that? I can hire this magician chappie from London. He's a whiz. He's so good, he'll make sure *only the Maguires* see him. He'll have the spirit voices telling 'em to take the first boat to the bally States, and they won't know whether they're coming or going."

"Is anyone *really* that good?" asked Cynthia. She waved her arm and knocked a cream bun on the floor. "Now look what I've done," she said indifferently. "Mucked up the old frump's carpet. Oh, well . . . where were we . . . ?"

"You were asking me whether he was any good?" scoffed Cuthbert. "The man's a genius. Why, Bertie Stuart-Graham hired him for a house party up in Scotland because he wanted revenge on some girl who wouldn't marry him. This magician chappie drove this girl to a complete nervous breakdown. Lord! How we all laughed when they carted her off."

Cynthia narrowed her eyes. "If I agree to

help you, how can I be sure you won't tell anyone of my part in it?"

"You can't," said Cuthbert, with a great shrug of his massive shoulders. "But what would it matter anyway? No one blamed Bertie for the girl's nervous breakdown. Everyone thought it the best joke in years."

A sudden vision of a quivering, terrified Molly rose before Cynthia's eyes. She gave Cuthbert a bewitching smile. "And what can I do?" she asked.

"Buy the girls a set of ghost stories. Real creepy ones like Sheridan Le Fanu and things like that. Talk a lot about ghosts. Tune up their minds, so to speak."

"I'll do it," said Cynthia. "And now let's ring the bell and get out of this gnome-ridden parlor."

Cuthbert rang the bell. The owner of the tea shop, a thin, faded lady, inappropriately called Mrs. Jolly, answered the summons.

She let out a mouselike squeak of dismay at the sight of the cream bun lying on the smart blue carpet that she had just bought at great expense. While Cuthbert searched for coins to pay the bill, Cynthia held Mrs. Jolly's eyes with her own. Then she looked down at the cream bun, taking Mrs. Jolly's gaze with her. Very slowly and deliberately, she raised her little French heel and ground the bun into the carpet.

Mrs. Jolly raised her hands to her face in dismay. The couple went out laughing heartily, and the sound of their laughter still rang in her ears as she bent over her precious rug and began slowly and painfully to remove the mess.

CHAPTER NINE

Cuthbert's home, called Hadding Court, seemed to be filled to overflowing with noisy young guests. Lord Toby Holden escaped into the gardens as often as he could, relishing in the tangled wilderness and having long enjoyable talks with the Postlethwaite's gardener, who seemed to have turned avoidance of work into a positive art.

As Cuthbert had expected, Lady Fanny had accepted his invitation with delight.

The Maguire sisters gloomily surveyed their new quarters and wondered over Lady Fanny's raptures.

The furniture in their suite was old and heavy and massive. Ivy blocked most of the view from the windows and a chill smell of damp and dry rot pervaded the whole house.

"It's like one of those places in those books Cynthia's been giving us to read," said Mary in an awed whisper.

"Don't talk in such a low voice. There's nothing to be afraid of," replied Molly in a bracing voice. "I told you not to read those books. You've had nothing but nightmare after nightmare. Any minute now you *will* start seeing ghosts. Why don't you go to your room and lie down before dinner?"

Mary would rather have stayed with her braver sister but did not want to say so. She trailed off reluctantly into her bedroom and without undressing climbed into a massive four-poster and lay staring up at the worn canopy with wide, frightened eyes.

She suddenly became aware that someone or something was watching her. She turned her head and stared across the bedroom and then put a hand to her mouth and made little choking noises of pure fright.

Standing, leaning against the wall, was a thin, cadaverous figure dressed from head to foot in black. He wore a black skullcap on his straggling gray hair and his eyes gleamed like wet stones in the dim light of the room.

Then he spoke. And that was worse than anything. His voice seemed to come from a long, long, way away: "Go back to where you came from. You are not wanted in England."

Mary found her voice and screamed and screamed and screamed. But when Molly, and practically everyone else in the castle, came rushing in, there was absolutely nothing to be seen. Molly began to wonder if the blow to Mary's head when she fell off the bicycle had addled her wits. After the others had left, shaking their heads and muttering their disbelief, Molly sat holding her sister's hand and worrying. Mary had been so definite and her voice was still trembling with fear. At last the shock and the sedative drink that Molly had given her began to take effect and Mary fell asleep.

Long shadows were falling across the unkempt lawns outside. Molly eased her hand free from Mary's and went softly to her room and sank into an easy chair by the window. Could someone be playing a terrible practical joke? But Molly found that she too had been influenced by the ghost stories she had recently read. She began to feel increasingly nervous. Far away, she could hear the sound of the dressing gong. Time to start the long preparations for dinner. She rose and crossed to the massive dressing table and sat down in front of it. Looking at herself in the mirror, she reached out her hand for her hairbrush, wondering why her maid, Goodge, had not appeared. The hairbrush was not in its usual place and, twisting around, Molly saw it lying on the floor. It must have fallen there when she had dashed to Mary's aid.

She picked up the brush and turned back to the mirror.

A horrible white graveyard face looked back at her from under a mop of black curls that seemed to be a parody of Molly's own. The thin white lips opened and a dreadful voice whispered, "Go away. Go back to America or your sister will die."

Molly fell backward in her fright and landed on the floor. Shaking in every limb, she picked herself up and bravely faced the mirror—and her own white face stared back at her.

With trembling hands she searched the face of the mirror and the back of the mirror and then sat down heavily, feeling all the hopelessness of complete despair and shock. Miss Molly Maguire was very, very frightened indeed.

Earlier that day Mrs. Pomfret put up the heavy shutters on the post office windows. The postmistress had planned to spend her half day resting in bed. She had felt very tired ever since the pageant and was suffering from a nagging pain in the small of her back. But her old friend, Mrs. Jolly, had written to invite her for tea. It would mean a long walk along the country roads in the heat but Meg Jolly's teas were worth a bit of effort and Meg Jolly's gossip was always worth listening to.

Mrs. Pomfret climbed upstairs to her small bedroom above the shop and took down her best straw hat. The sunlight shone into the room, highlighting the broken straw. Mrs. Pomfret gave a tired little sigh and wound her best scarf carefully around the crown in such a way as to hide as many of the holes as possible.

Outside the front door of the shop the heat struck her like a wave. People were saying the unnatural weather was all the fault of the government, but Mrs. Pomfret preferred to believe it was some kind of divine punishment for England's wrongs. Stories of the ill-treatment of the South African prisoners were only now beginning to appear in the newspapers, and what more fitting punishment than that England should be cursed with Africa's weather? She turned to lock the door and then noticed a round box sitting on the step. It was tied up with broad satin ribbons and had her name on it.

Her thrifty mind already registering that the ribbons would do to refurbish her Sunday dress, Mrs. Pomfret carried the box inside and carefully opened it. There, nestling on a bed of rose-colored tissue paper, lay a hat. And such a hat! It was of biscuit-colored straw, with a smart wide brim. The crown was decorated with artificial flowers, so beautifully made that they looked as if they had just been picked. With trembling hands, Mrs. Pomfret lifted the hat up and looked at the label. Paris!

There was a small note at the bottom of the box. It said, "A very happy Wednesday to Mrs. Pomfret, from Molly and Mary."

"God bless them," whispered Mrs. Pomfret, walking over to the mirror. She tossed her well-worn straw into the corner and, with reverent hands, placed the new hat on her head. Mrs. Pomfret no longer saw the lines on her face or the gray in her hair. She felt like a young girl again. The pain in her back seemed to have miraculously disappeared.

With her head held very high and feeling like Queen Alexandra, Mrs. Pomfret took the long road to Mrs. Jolly's, impervious to the heat or the miles. She seemed to float there under the shadow of that splendid hat.

There was a full half hour's discussion and wonder about the hat with Mrs. Jolly before both ladies gained enough breath to talk about other things.

"Do you see that faint mark on the carpet?"

asked Mrs. Jolly as she refilled the teapot.

Mrs. Pomfret looked down and then exclaimed in dismay, "Oh, your new rug, Meg. Customers are *so* careless!" Mrs. Pomfret was the only customer that day, as it was also Mrs. Jolly's half day and the CLOSED sign swung gently against the door.

"That," said Mrs. Jolly with dramatic relish, "was done *deliberate.*"

"*No!*"

"Fact. It was that Lady Cynthia who's staying with Lord and Lady Holden. She was in here with Mr. Postlethwaite and she dropped one of my best cream buns on the floor." Mrs. Jolly's voice trembled and her eyes filled with tears. "She—she called me—a—a *frump.*"

"Well, you're not," said Mrs. Pomfret gently. "Lady Cynthia always tells lies like that to be unkind. Why, you should hear what she says about my Miss Molly, and Miss Molly is much more beautiful, to my way of thinking, than Lady Cynthia. Do go on. What happened next?"

Mrs. Jolly leaned forward. "She stood up to leave and, while Mr. Postlethwaite was paying the bill, she *ground* the cream bun into my new carpet."

"Fancy!" cried the postmistress, shocked to the core.

"But that's not all," said Mrs. Jolly, beginning to cheer up in front of such an excellent audience. "I'll tell you what they were planning to do . . ." And dropping her voice to a whisper, she told Mrs. Pomfret all about the haunting of the Misses Maguire.

"Oh, dear," said Mrs. Pomfret, her eyes round with horror. "The girls are already at Hadding Court and goodness knows what may be happening to them." She got resolutely to her feet. "I must go and warn them immediately."

Lord David eyed Miss Molly Maguire across the dinner table. She was looking unusually white and nervous and her sister, Mary, seemed on the point of collapse. As the long meal went on he began to feel increasingly anxious. The girls usually exuded an atmosphere of excellent health and high spirits. Now Molly's face was so white it was practically translucent and she started at every sound.

He had been tempted to try out his Regency buck act with Molly and had already drooped his eyelids at her and tried out his mocking laugh, but Molly had only rather testily asked him if he had indigestion.

Cynthia was talking away in his ear, her high affected drawl grating on his nerves. Women used to have nice voices, thought Lord

David, remembering his mother. Now all the girls seem to copy their fathers' accents. And the latest baby talk was the end. "Is Davy cwoss wif ickle Cynthia?" remarked his beloved's voice. He was about to reply when his eye was caught by a movement outside the window. In the greenish twilight there seemed to be a window box moving up and down.

He looked again. The "window box" resolved itself into a smart hat with the faded and anxious face of the postmistress, Mrs. Pomfret, underneath.

Mrs. Pomfret seemed to be trying to catch Molly's attention but Molly was staring at the untouched food on her plate. Cynthia was still lisping away, demanding to know whether he were angry with her. "Of course not," he lied, getting to his feet.

"Where oo going?" asked Cynthia in surprise.

Lord David looked down at her, wondering for the hundredth time what he had ever seen in her. He said, "I am going to that small room —you know, the place that young ladies are not supposed to know about."

He moved hurriedly from the dining room and made his way through the hall and out into the garden. Mrs. Pomfret nearly jumped out of her skin when she turned and saw David standing behind her. She began to babble.

161

"Oh, dear, Lord David. I was just trying to catch Miss Maguire's eye."

"It must be something very important," said Lord David.

Mrs. Pomfret looked awkwardly at the ground. "Miss Molly asked me to find her a special kind of silk for her embroidery," she finally gasped.

"Come now," said Lord David soothingly, taking her by the arm and leading her away from the dining-room windows. "A lady like you, Mrs. Pomfret, does not come all this way to talk about silks. You must tell me the truth. Something has frightened Miss Molly badly."

Mrs. Pomfret let out a squeak of distress. "I must tell you then," she cried. "It has obviously started already."

Lord David steered her into a summerhouse in the gardens, out of the sight of the windows of the Court.

Straightening her hat with careful fingers, Mrs. Pomfret sat primly down on the edge of a cane chair while Lord David drew up another chair and sat opposite. And Mrs. Pomfret told him everything from the incident of the cream bun to the proposed haunting of Molly.

The windows of the drawing room opened and couples began to move about the terrace, chattering and laughing. "Dinner must be over," Lord David said. "I must go and tell Miss Molly before she decides to retire to her rooms. Don't worry, Mrs. Pomfret, everything will be all right." He gave a sudden infectious grin. "I say, what a stunning hat!" Mrs. Pomfret blushed like a girl and thanked him.

Then she got up to leave. "I am going to be cowardly, my lord, and slip away. I do not wish to make an enemy of Lady Cynthia. She could do me quite a lot of damage in the town. I am sorry to have to speak so about your fiancée, but my loyalties lie with Miss Maguire and her sister."

Lord David bit his lip in vexation. He longed to say that Cynthia no longer meant anything to him, but the evening had already been complicated enough.

Molly and Mary were seated quietly in a corner of the drawing room. The bright young things of the house party flitted endlessly to and fro. They kept throwing the girls sidelong looks and the air was electric with a kind of suppressed expectation.

Molly looked up nervously as she realized that Lord David was standing in front of her. "Would you care to take a turn in the garden, Miss Maguire?" he asked.

"The night air may be bad for your constitution, my lord," said Molly with a pathetic attempt at humor.

"My constitution never felt better," he said, raising her gently to her feet, "and Miss Mary must come, too. It is not often I have an opportunity to escort *two* beautiful girls." And talking light nonsense and teasing them gently, he led them out into the soft evening air and across the dew-laden lawns. Molly seemed to relax but Mary started and shied at every shadow.

Molly looked at him in surprise as he suddenly said in a very serious voice indeed, "Now we can talk. They are trying to frighten you away."

"They?" queried Molly faintly.

A little breeze rustled the leaves and every shadow of the garden seemed alive with menace. Far away, the sound of the sea whispered on the beach like the voices of the dead, murmuring and crying in the chains of their spirit world.

"I mean Cynthia and Cuthbert," said Lord David.

Molly took a deep breath and the color slowly returned to her cheeks. How pretty and romantic the overgrown garden suddenly seemed. And the voice of the sea only conjured up pictures of long, sunny summer days.

Lord David told her all about the plot—how the magician had been hired and how they planned to frighten her out of England.

Mary was beginning to look radiant. "I thought I was out of my mind," she said. "What shall we do to this magician?"

"*You* will not do anything," said Lord David firmly. "You must leave me to deal with it."

"Pooh!" said Molly rudely. "We want our revenge."

She paused for a minute, startled by the sudden memory of how she had wanted revenge on Lord David. How long ago that all seemed and how much seemed to have happened to her since then. She went on, "It's very kind of you to have warned us and it's awfully decent of Mrs. Pomfret to have come all this way, but we should get a bit of our own back."

Lord David grinned at the "awfully decent." Molly was becoming very anglicized in accent and speech. "Then let me come, too," he urged.

Surprisingly, Mary backed him up. "I really don't want to have anything to do with him, Molly," she pleaded.

Molly noticed Roddy hurrying across the gardens toward them and wondered if the presence of the marquess could have anything to do with her sister's sudden lack of spirit. But David was speaking again. "I'll go upstairs and hide myself in your room, Molly. You stay with the others until they all go upstairs to bed. Then we'll catch him together."

Roddy had joined them by this time and was

told the whole story. Mary should pretend to go to her room, he said, and he would take her for a walk in the gardens instead. Mary agreed enthusiastically and Molly gave a little sigh. Her sister was obviously in love with the marquess . . . but was the marquess in love with Mary?

She walked slowly back to the house with Lord David.

Lord David felt he had been waiting behind the curtain in Molly's room for hours. He had a sinking feeling that nothing was going to happen. Just as he was wondering whether to give up his vigil and join the others downstairs, he heard a board creak in the corridor outside and then there was silence. The door opened very slowly and quietly, and a dark figure that looked like an insubstantial black ghost crept into the room and moved behind the dressing table. Then there was a stealthy click—*His workbox*, thought David—and then silence again.

A long wait began, David leaning out of the window, hoping that the sound of his breathing would not carry to the magician.

He found himself hoping that the man would attack Molly so that he could pose as a hero.

Brisk footsteps came along the corridor, the

door swung open, and Molly's maid, Goodge, came in. She struck a lucifer and lit the gas lamps in their brackets, flooding the room with light, and then went out again.

For a few moments nothing happened. Peering through a chink in the curtain, Lord David saw the magician creep from behind the dressing table. He looked a frightening figure, even in the bright light, with his graveyard face and black wig.

He turned out all the lights except one that he lowered until the room was full of shadows. Then he took a hairbrush and some other items from the dressing table, placing them carefully on the floor, standing back to survey the effect, and then replacing them to make them look as if they had accidentally fallen to the floor.

Footsteps in the corridor again. *Pause . . . silence . . . wait.* The door swung abruptly open and Molly stood on the threshold. She moved into the room, stretched and yawned, and then looked around. It was so casual, so well done, that Lord David thought for a moment that Molly had forgotten all about the magician.

Molly sat down at the dressing table and looked at herself in the glass. With a little moue of irritation she turned around and saw the objects scattered on the floor and bent to retrieve them. With almost uncanny speed the "ghost" slipped out the mirror, replaced it with plain glass, and took up his position behind it. Molly returned to the dressing table and sat down. She looked long and hard at her "reflection." Then she leaned forward and took the "ghost's" nose firmly between finger and thumb and tweaked hard. There was an agonized yell. Lord David sprang from behind the curtains but the magician was quicker than both of them. He was out of the door and down the corridor before either of them had time to draw breath.

Molly made a move to run after him but David held her back. "Let him go," he said, trying to control his laughter. "What a splendid girl you are, you should have seen his face."

Molly burst out laughing as well and they clung together, bawling with mirth. Lord David suddenly became very conscious that he was holding Molly in his arms. She stopped laughing and looked up at him.

The hell with good form, thought Lord David savagely. He tilted up her chin and bent his mouth to hers.

For one startled moment Molly thought of pushing him away. Then her senses took over and her lips clung to his, and a tide of passion swept them both and left them shaking. Lord David was immersed in the feel of Molly, the scent of Molly, and the passion of Molly. In the dim light of the room he could see the beautiful curve of her breast above her gown. One tiny logical bit of his mind stared down at himself, muttering endearments as his mouth moved slowly down to that delectable bosom, and the rest of him didn't give a damn. His expert hands moved around to the fastenings at the back of her gown. She murmured a faint protest, but so faint he did not pay the slightest attention.

"David!"

The scandalized voice calling his name was not that of Molly but of Lady Cynthia, who was standing in the doorway and looking as if she couldn't believe her eyes. She had decided to visit Molly's room to gauge the amount of nervous damage done by the magician. She had expected to see a Molly Maguire trembling with fear but hardly a Molly Maguire trembling with passion.

Molly stood proudly beside Lord David, waiting for him to tell Cynthia that the engagement was at an end and that he and Molly were to be married. But all Lord David did was to say in a perfectly normal voice, "Oh, hello, Cynthia." He walked to the door, turned, and remarked gently, "Good night, Molly," and then, taking Cynthia by the arm, led her off down the corridor.

Miss Molly Maguire threw herself down on the bed and cried and cried. She cried because she was a foreigner, lost and at sea in a strange land where people drove each other mad for the fun of it and handsome lords could make love and walk away as casually as if they were leaving the breakfast table.

"Let's go into your sitting room, where we can talk in private," said Lord David.

"I have nothing more to say to you," snapped Cynthia.

"But I have a lot to say to *you*, dear Cynthia," he said, pushing open the door that led to her rooms and all but dragging her inside.

At the other end of the corridor Mary watched them with shock and dismay. She felt sure that her sister was falling in love with the handsome lord. She could have sworn Lord David loved Molly. It seemed as if it were all a sham. And she would have to tell her sister. Better that Molly should hurt now than suffer much more later.

"Of course I want you to release me from the engagement," Lord David was saying acidly. "I am not in the habit of making love to virgins unless my intentions are strictly honorable. I mean to marry Molly Maguire, and nothing you can say or do can stop me. You can hire as many magicians as you like, and I will still marry her."

"That was Cuthbert's doing," said Cynthia, turning an ugly color.

"I happen to know it was as much your doing as his," said Lord David.

Cynthia saw that the game was up but her mind was working feverishly. She needed just a little time.

"Well, it looks as if I have lost you," she said with a lightness she did not feel. "But it is all very humiliating. My parents will be most disappointed. I shall return to town tomorrow. But mother is not well at the moment, David, and this news would upset her terribly. Can you at least wait a fortnight and I'll tell her then? It will give me time to prepare her for the news. Please, David."

She looked very beautiful and appealing. And Lord David felt great relief that he was getting off so easily. He gladly agreed to her terms and then went off to search for Cuthbert's bedroom so that he might give that young gentleman the punch in the nose he so richly deserved.

CHAPTER TEN

Mrs. Pomfret returned slowly from her evening walk around the harbor. All did not seem to be going well with her heroine. Molly was looking tired and cross and changed the subject every time that nice Lord David's name was mentioned.

Her own life seemed to be looking up. One by one she had begun to buy the necessary essentials for her home, a thing she had never been able to do when she was paying blackmail money to Billy Barnstable. In another week she would have enough saved to buy a new dress. The week after that, new gloves. *And* the week after that, new boots, bright, shiny boots, with elastic sides and little high heels.

Her thoughts were still mostly on Molly, however, as she put the kettle on the stove to boil and took down a tin of biscuits from the shelf. Molly had left Cuthbert's, the morning following Mrs. Pomfret's warning, but she and Mary were no longer to be seen around on their bicycles and had not even called at the post office. Perhaps Lord David was a *philanderer*, just like one of those dreadful characters in Mrs. Henry Wood's books. Mrs. Pomfret was so engrossed with this new idea that she did not see the shadow falling across the kitchen window or hear the door being gently opened.

A low cough made her turn around, dropping the tin of biscuits in her fright.

Billy Barnstable was leaning against the doorjamb, a sheepish smile on his face.

"Here, now," he said, as the postmistress made terrified, choking noises in her throat. "I ain't going to hurt you. I've come to ask you a favor."

Mrs. Pomfret eyed the rifle propped against the kitchen wall and prayed for Molly Maguire's courage.

"What do you want?" she said faintly, while her heart was already mourning the loss of the dress, the gloves, the boots.

"I want peace and quiet and my old job back," said Billy, sitting down at the kitchen table. "I can't get work anywhere. Times are hard and I'm starving. I've been eating out of fields, whatever I could get. Blimey! I'm hungry, I am."

He picked up the tin of biscuits and looked at it longingly.

"They'll have me back at my old job," he said. "If I promise to behave meself, will you tell that Maguire female to leave me alone?"

"But you tried to kill her," screamed the postmistress, who had heard of the wire across the road.

"Naw!" said Billy. "Wanted to give her a tumble, that was all. Then she starts calling me names like you've never heard and I was mad and starving and went for her with the cudgel. For gawd's sake, believe me. You don't know what hunger does to a man."

"How can I believe you?" whispered Mrs. Pomfret. "Why should I? You sat there, week after week, watching me crying and taking my money, and you never had any pity."

Billy shifted awkwardly in his seat. "It seemed like a game to me," he said. "Easy pickings, you know. That's the way me Da brought me up. See your chance and take it, he allus said."

"Is your father alive?" asked Mrs. Pomfret.

Billy shook his head and soundlessly parodied a head being jerked in a noose.

"Well, there you are," said Mrs. Pomfret, regaining her courage. Dress, shoes, and gloves began to appear on a rosy horizon in her mind.

She opened the tin of biscuits and Billy stared at their brightly colored icing tops as if hypnotized and then tears began to run down his cheeks, cutting clean furrows on his dirty face.

"Go and wash your face and hands, Billy," said Mrs. Pomfret. "I have a piece of game pie in the larder and some bread and butter and you shall have it directly. Much better for an empty stomach than sugar biscuits."

While Billy washed at the kitchen sink, she put the wedge of pie and thick slices of bread and butter on the kitchen table. Billy fell on them, desperately trying to eat slowly, but ending up by cramming the food into his mouth with both hands.

When he had finally finished every last crumb, he looked at Mrs. Pomfret with shame-faced gratitude.

"I'd like for to say how I'm truly sorry," he mumbled.

"I shall trust you," said Mrs. Pomfret, her sensitive soul realizing the great effort it had cost the uncouth and rough Billy to choke out this apology. "Will you be able to get your room back at Mister Wothers's?"

Billy shook his head. "He's got another chap, and I ain't exactly popular around here."

Mrs. Pomfret wrestled furiously with her conscience. The vicar had said in church only last Sunday that one should truly forgive and help the repentant sinner.

"I have a little room upstairs," she said slowly. "But I do not know if I could take in a *man* lodger. What would the people in the town say?"

"They wouldn't say nuffink if we was married," said Billy suddenly.

Mrs. Pomfret raised her thin freckled hands to her suddenly hot cheeks. "The whole idea is ridiculous. I'm at least thirty years older than you! Now drink your tea and we'll pretend that you never said . . . er . . . what you did say."

She searched her mind feverishly for some change of subject. "Do you still read Westerns?" she asked.

"Haven't read one in weeks," said Billy. "Couldn't afford to buy 'em."

"There is a new one in by Art Rudge," said Mrs. Pomfret. "It's called *Shootin' Irons*." She passed the book over to Billy. "Who taught you to read?"

"Went to school till I was eleven," said Billy

proudly. "'Course, that was before me Da
. . ." Again his large hands parodied the hanging.

"Quite, quite," said Mrs. Pomfret hurriedly,
but Billy had opened the book and plunged in,
his lips soundlessly forming the words.

Mrs. Pomfret watched him, realizing with a
little shock that it was nice to have company,
even the silent company of her ex-blackmailer.

At one point Billy raised his head in the
slow manner of a large pig looking up from
its trough and said, "If we was married, you'd
have my pay same as your own," and went
back to reading.

The whole idea is so ridiculous, thought
Mrs. Pomfret. *Marry Billy, indeed!* "*But you
would be married, really married,*" whispered
a little imp in her ear. "*You've only been a
mistress before.*"

Mrs. Pomfret resolutely banished the imp
and rose and went to the stove to make a fresh
pot of tea.

Molly looked in surprise at Bobby and Jim
Wheelan. The twins had called at the Holdens
to present their usual bouquet of flowers, culled
from the neighboring gardens along the way.

"A *man,*" said Molly. "A *man* at the post
office? Are you *sure?*"

The twins nodded their heads energetically.

"Sure as sure," said Bobby. "Ma told me to go to the back door of the post office to see if Mrs. Pomfret would sell me some envelopes, even though the shop was closed.

"I knocked at the kitchen window and she came to the door, Mrs. Pomfret, I mean. And sitting at the table was this big chap a-reading a book."

"What did he look like?" asked Molly.

Bobby frowned. "He was old . . . looked like him," he said, pointing out of the window at one of the undergardeners.

Molly followed the direction of his grubby finger and her heart sank. For the particular undergardener that Bobby had singled out looked exactly like Billy Barnstable.

She came to a sudden decision. She had discovered that the villa boasted a gun room. She would find Lord Toby and turn the conversation around to guns. She would find out where he kept the key to the gun room and then, suitably armed, would descend on the post office after dark.

The thought of taking some action, however dangerous, was positively healing to the hurt she had suffered since her visit to Cuthbert's. She had gone out of her way to avoid Lord David. She had prayed and hoped to learn that his engagement had been broken but, although

179

Cynthia had returned to London, things in that direction seemed to be the same as ever. The sad result was that Mary had refused to see Roddy, condemning both Roddy and Lord David as a pair of heartless philanderers.

Accordingly, as soon as the twins had left, Molly ventured out into the garden to find Lord Toby. He was standing, berating his head gardener over the "depressing bally formality" of the whole place, and the Scottish gardener was grunting and refusing to take any notice.

Molly waited until Lord Toby retired, defeated.

To her dismay, Lord Toby refused to let her inspect the gun room. Ladies, he said firmly, knew nothing about guns and furthermore, he, Lord Toby, had such a beastly cold that he was going to lie down since Scottish gardeners were an invention of the devil and nobody cared whether he lived or died. So there!

Molly thought quickly. She had a plan. She knew it was wrong but Mrs. Pomfret's reputation must be saved at all costs. Sending up a small prayer for forgiveness, she told Lord Toby in warm, sympathetic, and cooing notes that she had just the thing to make him feel better. And she disappeared to her rooms for a few minutes and returned bearing a bottle of Maguires' Leprechaun Dew.

"Dear me," said Lord Toby, looking at the leprechaun. "What an evil-looking gnome."

"But it *works*," said Molly earnestly. "We wouldn't have made our fortune otherwise. It's not for children, you know. It's only sold to strong *healthy* people . . . I mean, healthy people with colds."

"I feel so bad I'll try anything," said his lordship. "Fancy me getting a cold in the middle of a heat wave. How much do I take?"

"Oh . . . a generous amount," said Molly, crossing her fingers behind her back.

"Then I won't need a spoon. Bottoms up!" said his lordship, tilting the contents down his throat.

Molly watched him anxiously. "Dear me!" said Lord Toby. "How very comforting! I feel quite well. I could dance."

He executed a few nimble steps across the lawn and was brought up short in front of a shell-bordered flower bed.

Lord Toby stared at it thoughtfully as if he had never seen it before. He slowly bent down and plucked out a shell and threw it over his shoulder. Then another. And then another. "It's beautifully simple," he murmured. "Never thought of it before. Don't like 'em? Throw 'em away."

He then began running madly from flower

bed to flower bed, until the air was full of a
sort of shell snowstorm. A posse of desperate
Scottish gardeners tried to restrain him but
Lord Toby seemed to have developed the
strength of ten men. "Hollyhocks. *Hate* hollyhocks!" he roared, plucking the offending flowers out by the bushel. One clump was particularly stubborn and he wrestled with it man-
fully until it came away all at once, catapult-
ing him across the lawn. His keys flew from his
pocket and fell on the grass. Molly picked
them up quietly and headed for the gun room.

Lord David sat slumped in an armchair beside his study window, staring unseeingly out
the open French windows at the garden. The
heat was suffocating and with an impatient
hand he wrestled with his necktie and threw
it across the room. Then he unfastened his
collar stud and the collar followed the necktie.
Was it some mad liberated American custom, he fretted, to allow a man to caress one
intimately and then look at him the next day
as if he had crawled out of a bit of old cheese?
It was humiliating. It was dreadful. He was a
fool to linger on here. Roddy also blamed him
for Mary's coldness and spent his days at the
top of the house quite blatantly spying on the
sisters next door. He came clattering into the

room with grating cheerfulness, shouting, "You'll never believe what's happening next door. Old Toby's gone off his rocker at last. Shouting and dancing and wrecking the garden. Lady Fanny comes out and tries to restrain him and he calls her a superannuated scout master!" Lord David looked at his friend with a dull eye.

"Don't care, eh?" said Roddy cheerfully. "Well, listen to the next bit of news. Molly picks up Toby's keys, which he dropped when he was cavorting around, and sneaks off to the gun room, which is on our side of the house. She takes down a whopping great rifle, cleans and loads it like an expert, and disappears out of the room with it. Next thing, she's skulking out of the house with a cloak on . . . a cloak in this weather, mind you, and heads for the town."

"What on earth is she up to?" said Lord David, jumping to his feet. "I'd better go after her. If I can't find her, I'll ask Mrs. Pomfret."

Molly hurried down toward the harbor. The heat was suffocating and humid. It was like walking through hot soup. Not a leaf stirred or a bird sang. The water lay in the harbor like black glass. Molly cursed herself for not having visited Mrs. Pomfret sooner. She had kept to the house like a wounded animal, nursing her hurt.

With a fast-beating heart, she crept along the side of the post office and looked in the kitchen window. Mrs. Pomfret was sitting in a rocking chair, sewing at some printed material that lay in her lap. Billy Barnstable was sitting at the kitchen table with his great head bent over a book.

Molly opened the kitchen door very, very quietly and leveled the gun at Billy's head.

Lookee here, pardner. I'm takin' all the gold mine for myself, and this here gun says there won't be no arguments, read Billy. This was a smashing book, reflected Billy. He could almost swear he had heard the sound of a rifle being cocked. Then he realized he had. He looked slowly around and found himself staring down the barrel of Molly's gun.

"It's all right," said Molly. "Stand well clear, Mrs. Pomfret. I'll handle this."

Mrs. Pomfret jumped to her feet with a shriek and to Molly's surprise she ran and stood between the gun and Billy. "Do not touch him!" she cried, quite in the manner of her heroines.

Molly put down the gun and looked at the postmistress, with her mouth open. There was a silence in the little kitchen. Far away the thunder growled and rumbled.

She found her voice at last. "Have you gone quite mad, Mrs. Pomfret?" she demanded. "This—this—man is a blackmailer and a murderer. What is the meaning of it?"

"He has repented," said Mrs. Pomfret. "And we are to be married. That's right, Billy, love, isn't it?"

Billy smiled sheepishly by way of answer and tugged his forelock.

"Married!" Molly's face was a mask of disgust. "*You* and—and—*that*—"

"Billy is a good boy," said Mrs. Pomfret with quaint dignity. "He has given me his word that he *will* be good. You've got to trust people, you know."

Molly was trembling with shock. There was a tremendous flash of lightning and then a terrific crash of thunder overhead and the rain began to thud down on the roof.

"Mrs. Pomfret!" said Molly in a voice like ice. "You are nothing but a dirty old woman."

Two spots of color burned on the postmistress's pale cheeks.

"And you are a silly and cruel little girl, Miss Maguire. The next time I see you I hope to receive your apology. Please leave." Mrs. Pomfret held open the kitchen door. Molly stumbled out into the storm, which was lashing ferociously at the deserted streets.

Tears ran down her cheeks and mingled with

the rain. She felt very young and very alone. She thought longingly of Brooklyn and cursed the day she and Mary had ever concocted Maguires' Leprechaun Dew. Had it not been for that dreadful cough mixture, then she and Mary would be snug in Fulton Street.

She missed the life of Brooklyn, the hotchpotch of races, the feeling of being part of one of the youngest and most exciting cities in the world. *It would surely be easier to deal with the Chinese,* thought Molly furiously, *than these wretched English, with their rigid code of modes and manners.*

She was so engrossed in her misery that she bumped straight into Lord David, who was standing directly in her path.

He held out his hand. "The gun, Miss Maguire," he demanded.

"Take your hands off it, or I'll bean you with it," said Miss Maguire savagely, making the long mental return from Brooklyn.

He held a large silk umbrella over her head. She did not look at all beautiful with her face twisted up with rage and her hat a wreck but he loved her. So he took her by the arm and tried to lead her gently up the road. The noise of the storm was immense. Great peals of thunder rent the heavens and shook the earth. The sea boiled on the shore and jagged lightning lit up the hellishly moving restless scene of swaying trees and surging water.

They walked silently side by side about six feet apart. He had tried to shelter Molly with the umbrella but every time he approached her she looked as if she would jump into the sea.

As they approached his villa, which was just before the Holdens', he decided that he would have to kidnap Miss Molly Maguire. He could not possibly let her go home on her own in this state of wet and misery.

Luck was with him at the gates of his villa. A carriage came clattering along the road and Molly was forced to move onto the narrow pavement close beside him. Before she realized his intent he had tossed his umbrella into the bushes, swept her up in his arms, and started running with her to the house, seemingly oblivious to the hard punches she was delivering to his face.

Roddy was standing in the hall, staring in amazement. David dismissed him with a jerk of his head and carried the still struggling Molly into the drawing room. He put her down gently and then dodged as she swung another punch at his face. "I hate you . . . hate you *all*," she was gasping.

"You will sit down—wet as you are—and you will not leave this house until you have told me what is the matter. I find you walking along in the pouring rain, clutching a game rifle, and looking like death." His voice became very gentle. "I love you, Molly. Trust me."

"Why should I trust anyone, particularly you?" said Molly, trying to wring the water out of her dress. "You left my arms and went straight to Cynthia's bedroom."

"I went to Cynthia's *private sitting room* to tell her I had discovered the trick she had played on you and to tell her—"

He bit his lip. He had promised Cynthia faithfully that he would tell no one of their broken engagement until the fortnight was up. He had promised himself that he would tell Molly then. His promise would end on the night of an end-of-the-summer ball to be given for the girls by Lady Fanny. "You must trust me," he finished lamely.

Molly looked at him in contempt. "You English!" she spat out. "Saying one thing and meaning the other." She found herself telling him the whole story of Mrs. Pomfret, only leaving out the fact that Mrs. Pomfret had not been married.

"You are very young," said Lord David gently and then went on hurriedly for fear he might have sounded patronizing. "One doesn't give up longing for love and companionship simply because one is no longer young. You talk like a fool, Molly. If sex is not a dreadful and dirty thing for the young, why should it be disgusting in the old? You owe Mrs. Pomfret an apology. Billy may be crude and vulgar, but I should think Mrs. Pomfret enjoys having someone to mother. She must be lonely and she could not, of course, live with him under any different terms. Love has many faces, Molly. If you do not understand love, how on earth can you understand my love for you? I hardly understood it myself. I had not really been in love before."

She remained silent, staring down at the floor, the rainwater from her hat trickling down her face like tears.

"I have something planned for the night of your ball, Molly," he went on gently. "Will you trust me until then? Is it so much to ask? I have given someone my promise and I am bound by it up till then. Now, come along and I will take you home. But trust me . . . just a little."

Molly looked shyly up into his face. He looked very serious and there was an almost pleading look in his eyes.

Slowly she put out her hand. "I will try one more time," she said in a low voice. "I will trust you till then."

CHAPTER ELEVEN

Miss Molly Maguire stepped into her long French corset with the frivolous little eau de nil roses on the garters and turned around so that Goodge could tie the laces.

The long hot summer had finally ended and already a chill wind was blowing banks of dirty gray clouds across the sky and sending the first dead leaves fluttering to the ground.

Fires had been lit in all the rooms and the villa smelled pleasantly of beeswax and woodsmoke. In the ballroom at the back of the house the musicians were already tuning up. Somewhere along the corridor her parents and Bernie Abrahams were also getting ready for the ball. Molly felt a twinge of unease. Her father's "English" accent seemed even more peculiar now that she was able to compare him with the real thing.

Bernie was refreshingly the same as ever: loud, noisy, cocky, and perfectly prepared to compete with his English rivals for Molly's affections. Mrs. Maguire was now thin to the point of emaciation and very overwhelmed at the honor of living in a "real titled lady's home." She overtipped the servants and kept apologizing for her very existence and rejoiced the heart of the housekeeper, Mrs. Barkins, who had at last found someone to bully, realizing shrewdly that the more she bullied Mrs. Maguire, the more Mrs. Maguire tipped.

Mary came running in, looking radiant. She had been a changed girl since Molly had told her of the odd conversation with Lord David. "He *is* right!" Mary had cried. "We must trust them—David and Roddy, I mean." But she was just as shocked as Molly over the news of Mrs. Pomfret.

Mary was wearing her black hair dressed low on her forehead in the current fashion, but Molly had hers swept severely back from her brow and pinned in a top knot of curls which cascaded down the back of her head to her shoulders.

Mary was dressed in white chiffon trimmed with blue forget-me-nots. It was cut low to show her bosom to advantage and had masses of swirling chiffon skirts over taffeta petticoats.

Molly had chosen a severe gown in dull-red silk, falling from a low neckline to the floor in straight medieval lines. The sleeves were tight and long, ending in pointed cuffs. Lady Fanny had lent her a heavy ruby necklace set in antique gold. She had never looked more magnificent.

Lady Cynthia thought so as she watched the entrance of the Maguire sisters. This was her last chance for revenge and a weapon had unexpectedly been put into her hands by the arrival of the Maguire parents.

She endured the sight of Molly floating in the arms of Lord David, biding her time, and counting the minutes until the bell would be rung for supper.

Supper was in the form of a buffet in a large room adjoining the ballroom. Bernie was already there, holding forth to a large party of giggling debutantes, when Molly arrived on the arm of Lord David. The young people had obviously been drinking too much. The Maguire sisters were no longer a novelty, but Bernie and the Maguire parents were, and Molly saw at a glance that the bored socialites were hell-bent on mischief.

Thankfully Bernie was impervious to insult. He told corny jokes, he stuck his thumbs in his waistcoat, he roared and laughed. He told the company at large that he hoped to be married to Molly. Molly was irritated because Lord David obviously did not believe a word of it. Young people began throwing pellets of bread at each other and shouting from table to table.

Mrs. Maguire was shocked and distressed. This was not the way she expected English society to behave and said so to her husband, trying to shout above the noise. Unfortunately there was one of those deadly hushes in the conversation and Mrs. Maguire's voice rang across the supper room with dreadful clarity.

Cynthia's high drawl dropped into the silence following Mrs. Maguire's remark like acid.

"It's a good thing we've all been drinking champers and not that filth—what is it?—Maguire's Leprechaun Dew."

"Do you know," Cynthia went on, "I had a bottle of that cough syrup analyzed and it's one-hundred-and-forty proof alcohol! What a terrible country America must be. Why, you could kill little children with a cough syrup like that!"

"That's one of the *old* bottles," said Bernie hotly. "Stuff's as safe as mother's milk, now. We withdrew all the strong stuff from the market. Anyway, who are you to talk, sweetheart? The way you've been sinking the stuff you'd think you'd gotta hose in your left evening shoe."

"Really," gasped Cynthia. "Know your place, my good man."

"You can't put me in my place," grinned Bernie, "cos I ain't got one to be put into."

"Have you tried Sing Sing?" asked Cuthbert in a conversational voice. "Damned racketeers all you bally American chappies. Thank God for old England, that's what I say."

There was a murmur of agreement. Quite a lot of the young men had been rejected by the Maguire sisters and quite a lot of the young ladies were jealous.

But the whole thing would have passed over had not Mr. Joseph Maguire decided to make a speech. As snazzily dressed as a New Orleans riverboat gambler, complete with frilled shirt and a plethora of rings, Mr. Joseph Maguire addressed the startled guests.

In what he fondly imagined to be the very best of English accents, he began: "Folks. Youse have all got it wrong. Me and my lady wife are as English as the next man. Why, just listen to my voice. What-ho! Toodle-pip and all that." He gave a fat laugh. Nobody joined in but Bernie, who was leaning back in his chair, his little eyes twinkling with glee. "Atta-boy, Joe," he cheered.

"Now it seems that my lovely daughters what

I brung up good are to marry into the arrerstocracy. Not that one young man has asked me permission yet but I knows the love light in a chap's eyes when I sees it." He gave Lord David a broad wink. Molly was dying by inches in her chair and did not see Lord David wink back.

"Sit down," pleaded Mrs. Maguire. "Everyone's laughing at you." She held a wisp of handkerchief to her brow in what she fondly hoped was a genteel way.

"Sit down," Cynthia suddenly mimicked, ruthlessly copying Mrs. Maguire's gestures. "Everyone's laughing at you."

The company roared with delight as Mr. Maguire looked stupidly around like a large bull at the sound of two wives.

That did it. The young things had found a new sport. It was open season on Americans.

Catcalls, jeers, bread-throwing surrounded the bewildered Mr. Maguire. He looked slowly down at his wife, who was in tears, and then at Cuthbert Postlethwaite, who was laughing the hardest. He walked slowly toward Cuthbert and stood behind that young man's chair. He gently picked up the huge Cuthbert as if he were no more than a rag doll, and with one massive sweep of his great arms, threw Cuthbert through the French windows and into the garden. Fortunately for Cuthbert the windows were open, but unfortunately the gardeners had been re-edging the flower beds and he landed on a border of razor-clam shells like a ton of bricks.

Molly sat in a daze of pain and hurt. Lord David was laughing at her father, great tears of mirth rolling down his face. He recovered and was about to turn to Molly and say, "Your father is absolutely splendid, Molly, I'm going over there to shake him by the hand," when Molly walked away—over to where a large jelly stood quivering on a sideboard. She picked it up very carefully, walked over to Cynthia, and placed the bowl of ice-cold jelly upside-down tenderly on top of Cynthia's immaculate coiffure.

The guests came out of their state of shock and joined battle. Lady Fanny screamed and wept as ice cream, lobster patties, cream cakes, and the rest of what had been a sumptuous buffet went flying around the room.

It was a long time before the guests realized they were fighting each other.

The Maguire family—and Bernie—had gone.

A thin, watery sunlight broke through the clouds as the good ship *Titania* eased its way out from Southampton docks.

"Good-bye, England!" said Molly viciously.

"I hope I never set foot in this cursed country again."

A thin drizzle was still falling. Mrs. Maguire had gone to lie down in her cabin and was watched over anxiously by her husband.

Bernie, having ascertained that Molly would not consider marrying him, had cheerfully turned his attention to the prettiest girls on board.

The ship moved farther away.

"Look!" cried Mary. "Oh, look!"

The town band of Hadsea had rapidly debouched from a charabanc and were plunging into the resounding strains of "Rule Britannia." It seemed to be the only tune they knew. Two little boys, recognizable even in the widening distance as Bobby and Jim Wheelan, were hoisting a banner in front of the crowd of townspeople. "What does it say, Molly?" gasped Mary. "I can't read. I'm crying."

Molly read slowly, "It says, GOOD LUCK TO THE MAGUIRES. COME BACK HOME SOON."

Molly felt her own eyes fill with tears. The townspeople cheered and waved and she suddenly found herself cheering and waving back.

"There's Mrs. Pomfret . . . and Billy, I do declare," said Mary, wiping her streaming eyes.

The girls waved and waved until they could no longer see the figures on the dock.

"Well, I *never*," said Molly Maguire, wiping

her own eyes. "It just goes to show. I don't think we ever really knew them."

"It was so lovely," said Mary. "The whole town must have been there."

The whole town, except two certain gentlemen, thought Molly, with a wrenching wave of sadness. "They've probably forgotten we exist," she said. Mary nodded her head sadly. She did not even have to ask who Molly meant by "they."

"Well, that's that," said Roddy, turning away. "I still think we should have gone down to the front of the dock and waved or something."

"Why?" asked Lord David moodily. "Take it from me, dear boy, our romances were never meant to blossom. Of all the dashed self-sufficient girls. . . . Not an ounce of understanding for other people in her whole makeup. And she was downright cruel about poor Mrs. Pomfret. Look at the old Dowager Marchioness of Blexley. She married a young chap only this year."

Roddy looked at his friend uneasily. "It's not quite the same, you know," he ventured. "That sort of thing always went on in our set. It's different for people like Mrs. Pomfret. I mean, it's scandalous somehow."

"Snob!"

"Well, it is . . . different, I mean," said Roddy stubbornly. "That old postmistress will come to grief. The townspeople don't like it one bit. She'll lose her job."

Both men had remained at the back of the crowd of townspeople as the boat bearing the sisters back to America had sailed away. Both felt obscurely that they should have done something more dramatic.

"It wouldn't have worked," said Lord David gloomily. "Too much difference in race and culture."

"What? Mrs. Pomfret and Billy?"

"No, you ass! Us and the Maguires."

"It's that difference that's so intriguing," said Roddy. "There's a freshness, a charm, a—"

"Shut up. There's nothing we can do about it now. Anyway, think of all the times you've been in love. You'll fall for someone by next week. You usually do."

Roddy eyed his tall friend out of the corner of his eye. There were times when Lord David made him feel as if he, Roddy, were back at school, tagging along at David's heels and hanging on the older boy's every word. He felt a little spark of rebellion. He no longer knew whether he was in love with Mary or not. All he knew was he had never felt so miserable or lost in his life.

Lord David swung himself into his new toy—a Lanchester automobile. He had fondly imagined bowling along the country roads with Molly Maguire, watching the sun on her hair and listening to the fascinating twang of her American accent. But the Maguires had gone and taken the summer with them.

"Never mind," he said to Roddy. "Think how super London will look after Hadseal!"

But somehow the wretched Maguires seemed to have tainted London as well. The prettiest of debutantes seemed insipid, the wittiest of remarks, mere social posturing.

His flat in town looked dark and gloomy and overly masculine, with its heavy mahogany furniture and framed hunting prints. Every morning he flicked hurriedly through his mail, looking for an American postmark and feeling weary and dejected when there was none.

After two months had passed since the Maguire sisters' departure, he noticed with an almost clinical interest that the pain had not lessened. He had not seen Roddy for some time and began to wonder if his friend were avoiding him.

One of the least pleasant reminders of the summer, he reflected, was that Jennifer Strange girl, who seemed to have an uncanny knack of popping up like a rabbit every time he set a foot outside his door. Girls like Jennifer, thought Lord David sourly, positively seemed to relish being trodden on. The worse the snub or set-down, the more devoted she seemed to become.

His reverie was broken by the entrance of his man, who informed him that "two persons were desirous of seeing him."

"I would have turned them away, my lord," said the gentleman's gentleman with awful hauteur, "but the female person claimed acquaintanceship with you, my lord. Said she met you last summer."

Lord David's harsh features softened in an almost angelic smile. "Show her in, man. Show her in!" he cried.

He should have known it wouldn't be Molly, he thought dismally, as a shrinking Mrs. Pomfret was ushered in, followed by the lumbering bulk of Billy.

"Oh, my lord," twittered Mrs. Pomfret. "So kind. I had no one else to turn to. People are *awful*. . . ." Here she burst into noisy tears, while Billy stood on one foot and grinned and looked vacantly around the room.

"Here, now," said Lord David, ringing the bell and ordering tea and smelling salts. "You shall have some refreshment and then you will tell me all about it."

He waited patiently until the distressed postmistress had blown her nose and taken several gulps of tea. "I just *had* to ask for help, my lord. They have taken my job away from me!"

Lord David waited patiently until the next paroxysm of sobs had died away. "What happened?" he asked gently.

Piecing together Mrs. Pomfret's disjointed speech, he gathered that the townspeople did not approve in the least of her proposed marriage. They had been looking for an excuse to get rid of her and finally found one. Old Mr. Apple, who had delivered the post for half a century, was due to retire. She had suggested that Billy should have the job. The townspeople had managed to get Mr. Apple to write a letter to the postal department, complaining that he was being ousted from his job.

"So I lost mine," hiccuped Mrs. Pomfret. "They would not even see me at the head office. What am I to do? I don't want charity, my lord. I know Miss Maguire would have helped me and I was going to write to her, but then I saw that item in the social column of the *Daily Mail*. Poor girl. Poor, poor girl. So I—"

"*What!*" yelled Lord David.

"Now I-I've made you angry," wailed Mrs. Pomfret. Up came the handkerchief and out came the sobs.

Lord David turned in exasperation to Billy. "What's all this about? I mean—what's happened to Miss Maguire?"

"Dunno!" said Billy laconically, looking out the window.

Lord David set himself feverishly to calming Mrs. Pomfret again and drew the story from her bit by bit.

The Maguires were ruined. Faulty speculations on Wall Street had taken every penny of their fortune, but the newspaper article had not said what had become of them.

Lord David sat very still. Yellow fog was pressing itself against the window panes and the high metallic pipe of a starling seemed to intensify the cold of the winter's day outside. A coal shifted and fell on the hearth and he realized Mrs. Pomfret was saying something about America.

"Billy's ever so keen on Westerns and he's a *good* worker and I thought, my lord, since various titled gentlemen have been buying *ranches* in the states, perhaps you know of someone who would be willing to employ Billy."

Lord David swung around to look at Billy Barnstable. "Do you agree with this idea, Billy?"

"Sure," grinned Billy, twirling two imaginary shooting irons. "Pow! Pow!"

"I think it could be arranged," said Lord David slowly. "And you must allow me to pay your fare. No! I insist. Come back at the same time tomorrow and I will let you know what I have arranged. May I have a word with you in private, Mrs. Pomfret?"

She twittered and fussed over Billy, straightening his tie and pulling down his jacket, before she allowed him to be led away.

Lord David settled back in his chair and tried to push the picture of a starving and destitute Molly from his mind.

"Ah, Mrs. Pomfret," he said, searching for the right words. "Are you *sure* this is a good idea of yours? The wild West is not the same country that Billy finds in his books. He will find it very rough—hard work and long hours."

"I have great faith in Billy," said Mrs. Pomfret proudly. "I am not afraid of going to a new country. I am sure it will all be very exciting. In *Sage Sunset* the heroine, Annie Mac-Pherson, is a simple country girl from England and she copes marvelously. 'You gotta learn to shoot straight and hold your head high in this here country,' she says, tossing her russet hair from her eyes and looking across the sage brush. Now, I am not *young*, my lord, and my hair is gray, but it is still quite the same thing, is it not?"

"Quite," said Lord David, thinking that Mrs.

Pomfret might come up against some bad shocks. But she seemed determined to go through with her marriage to Billy, and the chap was a farm worker, after all.

"So long as you know what you are doing," he said heavily. "I shall see you tomorrow."

He waved aside her frantic thanks, desperate to get rid of her so that he could turn his mind to the problem of Molly.

After Mrs. Pomfret had twittered her way out, he seized his hat and cane and headed for his club in St. James's.

He found the Marquess of Leamouth buried in the depths of an armchair, a copy of the *Daily Mail* lying open on the table in front of him.

"Heard the news?" asked Lord David, taking the chair opposite.

Roddy nodded. "Happens to a lot of these American big shots," he said indifferently. "One minute they're all over the Riviera and the next minute they sink without a trace."

Lord David examined the great ache in his own heart with the clinical detachment of a surgeon and looked at his friend with some surprise. "And?" he demanded.

"And what?" said Roddy. "I say, have you seen the latest beauty, Deborah Willinton-James? Tremendous girl. Biggest eyes you've

206

ever seen and a magnificent pair of shoulders. I met her . . ."

Lord David's thin black brows snapped together and his long mouth was set in a hard line. "I should have known," he said bitterly. "You've got a heart like a damned butterfly, and I'm dashed well not going to sit here listening to you waffling on about some bally little society tart."

He strode from the room, snatching his hat and cane from the cloakroom on the way out and muttering curses under his breath.

He, Lord David Manley, would settle Mrs. Pomfret's boring problem by purchasing her steamship tickets at the shipping office, and while he was there he would damn well purchase one for himself and then he would scour every street in New York City for Miss Molly Maguire and he would drag her back to England by the hair if need be.

Roddy stood at the window of the club and watched the tall figure of his friend striding off into the fog. He was glad to see him go. He did not want any more lectures on the fickleness of his heart. He did not want his somewhat overpowering friend to know that only that morning he had rushed out and impetuously bought a steamship ticket.

Molly was able to take care of herself. But

Mary! He thought of Mary's fragile beauty. He thought of her penniless in the midst of that terrifying city and he hoped to God he could get there before it was too late.

Jennifer Strange waited until Lord David had left the steamship ticket office and then went in. Yes, said the fussy little clerk, his lordship had just bought a ticket for the liner *Triton*, which was sailing tomorrow. Did miss want a ticket also? No, miss did not. She wanted to go home that minute and write to Molly Maguire. Jennifer had an American friend in Brooklyn Heights, who, she felt sure, would find Miss Maguire's address and make sure the letter was delivered. It was the least she could do!

CHAPTER TWELVE

"Where on earth have you been, girl? Of all the stupid days to take time off. I declare I don't know what servants are coming to."

"The snow is falling quite heavily," said Miss Mary Maguire. "I'm sorry, ma'am."

"Sorry! You'll be a lot sorrier, my girl, if you do anything to wreck my dinner party," snapped Mrs. Carter III. "This is the most important evening of my life. Go to Jenkins immediately and he will tell you your duties."

Mary reflected dismally that she had not expected *Americans* to treat their servants so. In retrospect, Lady Fanny's army of servants seemed to have led a life of luxurious ease.

She had accepted the position of parlormaid

in Mrs. Carter's Brooklyn Heights' mansion because she had fondly remembered parlormaids as being somewhere quite high up the servants' social scale. But they always seemed to be three mysterious servants short and the job was a long, long day of heavy labor, performing the duties of housemaid, scullery maid, kitchen maid, and parlormaid all rolled into one. It was always, "Just fill in for today, Mary, until Beth . . . or Amy . . . or Maggie comes back." But the missing servants never materialized, and the heavy work went on.

She walked down the steps to the servants' quarters to find, to her surprise, that the black cook had been supplanted by a French chef and two assistants. Jenkins, the butler, looked up as Mary came in.

"Thank God you're back. Nearly lost your job. But I put in a word for you." Jenkins was always "putting in a word" for Mary, and Mary had initially been grateful to him until she had realized that Mrs. Carter III would never fire a parlormaid who did so much work for such low pay. The servants in the neighboring brownstones had often urged Mary to find a more comfortable position. But Mary was afraid that a lessening of work would mean an increase of heartache.

"What's all the fuss?" she demanded, taking a clean cap and apron out of the cupboard. "I didn't mean to be late. But the snow's falling like anything, and all the traffic and everything's jammed up along Fulton Street."

"Good," said Jenkins with gloomy relish. He was a thin, cadaverous New Englander who seemed to thrive on disaster. "Maybe his lordship won't turn up and it'll serve her right."

"His *lordship?*" queried Mary, her heart giving a painful lurch.

"Some marquess that Mister Carter met on the boat over," said Jenkins. "You've turned as white as a sheet, Mary. Sit down and have a cup of coffee. I can't have you ill on a night like this. Ma Carter's in a great flutter. She's been on the telephone all afternoon, bragging and bragging."

"What marquess? I mean—what's his name?" said Mary faintly.

"Dunno," said Jenkins. "Some old geezer with the gout probably."

"Probably," said Mary, the color slowly returning to her pallid cheeks.

"Now remember," said Jenkins. "You're to help me serve. And no daydreaming or dropping things. Finish that coffee and get ready to stand in the hall with me to take their coats."

Mary drank her coffee slowly. What a long, long time seemed to have passed since the summer in Hadsea. She could still see Bernie's waving arms, see his angry face. Sales of Maguire's Leprechaun Dew had dropped off almost entirely but the Maguire investments had been sound. Bernie had discovered on his return that Joseph Maguire had decided to handle the family fortunes himself, and several shrewd gentlemen on Wall Street had made their fortunes by selling the gullible Mr. Maguire everything from oilless desert tracts in Arizona to nonexistent mines in Bolivia. By the time the debts were paid off, the Maguires were worse off than they had ever been. Bernie had vowed to wash his hands of the whole family but had relented enough to set Molly up with her own dress shop in Fulton Street. Mary had surprised them all by refusing to join Molly. Her sister was too bitter about the subject of the English, and Mary preferred to cling to her dream that one day the marquess would come to find her.

Mrs. Carter erupted into the kitchen, a miracle of whalebone corsets and purple silk. Her massive bosom was thrust so far out in front and her large silk-encased bottom pushed out so far behind that she looked as if she was always just on the point of falling over. Her small snapping eyes darted to where the dreamy-eyed Mary was sitting at the kitchen table.

"Get to work this minute," roared Mrs. Carter. "And put *all* your hair under your cap."

Honestly, the girl was really too attractive to be a good servant.

A few minutes later and Mary was standing nervously in the hall behind Jenkins. One by one the dinner guests began to arrive. Mary began to relax. The same old faces. Mr. and Mrs. Pfeiffer—beer—the Hambletons—railroads—the Cunninghams—*old* money—and the Haagens—timber. All seemed nervous and excited and the conversation in the overstuffed drawing room, with its red plush chairs and heavy velvet curtains, centered on whether Mr. Carter III would bring his social prize home through the snow.

The penny-pinching Mrs. Carter had put herself out with unaccustomed extravagance for the occasion, although only the servants knew that the rented gold plate would go back in the morning along with Mrs. Carter's rented diamonds, rented chef, and rented hothouse flowers.

Outside there was the sudden slam of an automobile door, and the feathered headdresses of the ladies bristled with anticipation.

Jenkins left Mary with the drinks trolley and moved nimbly into the hall. Mr. Carter's booming voice . . . a light, pleasant English voice in reply. Mary found her gloved hands were shaking and put them behind her back.

Roddy, Marquess of Leamouth, drifted into

the room and into a rapturous welcome. His curls shone like burnished gold. He had lost his summer tan and his handsome face was thin and white. He chatted amiably in his pleasant drawl. Yes, America was a tremendous place. What filthy snow! Was it always like this? And Mrs. Carter's eyes glistened with triumph. These people were the *crème de la crème* of Brooklyn Heights' society. They had hitherto ostracized the pushing and grasping Mrs. Carter. But this stroke of fortune, this handsome marquess, had brought them home to roost in her drawing room. She plied Roddy with drink while her bosom swelled like the sail of a tea clipper in a high gale.

Mary stared at Roddy as if mesmerized. Only once did he look at her. One blue eye glanced briefly in her direction and then looked quickly away. Anger drove the tears from Mary's eyes. He was not going to recognize her!

As if in a dream, she helped Jenkins serve at table, wondering whether one could die from an excess of humiliation.

"Tell me, dear Marquess," said Mrs. Carter, with a roguish twinkle, "why are you not married?"

"What a simply excellent chef you have," said Roddy politely. But Mrs. Carter had been snubbed by coarser ways than the marquess had ever dreamt of and charged on regardless.

She gave the frozen-faced Roddy a naughty wink and poked him in the ribs with her fan. "We're all waiting, my lord. Why haven't you made some nice girl happy?"

"You must tell me more about the business world here, Mister Carter," said Roddy pleasantly. "It sounds fascinating."

Mr. Carter cast his wife an anguished look and chewed the ends of his mustache. The other guests shifted restlessly and began to wish—marquess or no marquess—that they had not come. Bessie Carter was the *end*!

Mrs. Carter's small eyes narrowed as Roddy was besieged with Wall Street information and everyone began to talk at once, very loudly and quickly. She was not used to having her will crossed. She quickly toted up in her cash-register mind the exact cost of the evening. Her aristocratic guest *would* sing for his supper. She was paying for it, after all. Her loud voice flattened over the conversations like a steam-roller.

"Don't be coy with me, Marquess. I insist on knowing why a handsome young lord like you is not married."

The other guests held their breath. They prayed for Bessie Carter's downfall and at the same time they dreaded it. Roddy put down his fork and stared at his plate. Then he raised his eyes and looked to where Mary was standing in the shadows of the room; her white face and frilly cap seemed to float, disembodied in the corner. The wind howled down the river outside with a great moaning yell and then died away, leaving the room in utter silence except for the crackling of the fire.

"I'll tell you," said Roddy quietly, keeping his eyes fixed on Mary's face.

"I had always fancied myself in love but I always got over it very quickly. Then a friend of mine invited me down to an English seaside resort. There were two American heiresses who needed taking down a peg, he said. It looked like good sport. Well, I fell in love with the younger. But I did not trust my own feelings. You see, I had been in love before.

"She left. I found I missed her frightfully. I heard she had lost her money and was working in New York. I came to find her . . . just to see her again.

"Now, by all the canons of good taste, I could not visit a house and propose to one of the servants. I felt that just to be near her would be enough. But it is not. Neither do the strict rules of good form seem to apply in this house, Mrs. Carter. I am saying in front of you all that I love her and want to marry her, and I want her to take off that ridiculous cap and take my arm and walk out of the house with me."

Mrs. Haagen gave a nervous titter. Mr. Carter looked nervously at Roddy's empty glass and decided it should not be refilled. Mrs. Carter looked disappointed.

"Oh, a *fairy* story," she cried.

Everyone plunged into conversation to cover the embarrassment engendered by the young lord's eccentricity and only Mary, standing in the shadows, heard the soft whisper, "Will you, Mary?"

She gave a funny, jerky little bob of her head. He rose slowly from the table and laid his napkin carefully beside his plate. He was unaware of the faces of the guests turned upward to him. He moved around the table and crossed the room to where Mary was standing.

He looked down at her, noticing the taut lines of strain on her face and the shadows of weariness under her large eyes.

"Will you?" he said again very softly, watching the warmth and love suddenly transforming her face. He gently unfastened the little lacy cap from her head. He put his arms around her and held her very close.

"This is madness!" spluttered Mrs. Carter III.

Unheeding, the couple were moving dreamily to the door. Hatless and coatless, they wandered out into the snowy streets of Brooklyn Heights.

The guests were bunched on the doorstep, staring after them openmouthed. Mary was laughing at something the marquess was saying and little feathers of snow sparkled in her hair.

Then the marquess bent his head and kissed her while Mrs. Carter trembled with cold, rage, and astonishment on her front doorstep.

One by one the guests began to leave.

They had never liked Bessie Carter anyway.

Miss Molly Maguire bent her head over her account books and sighed, and the wind whipping along Fulton Street sighed in answer. The shop was doing well. She had already been able to engage two assistants and soon she would be able to pay Bernie back. She kept one set of accounts for Bernie and another for her father. Joseph Maguire haunted the stock exchange, dreaming of making a killing. "I shall invest your money for you, Molly," he had promised, and Molly had promptly worked on a false set of books to show that Maguire Modes was running at a perpetual loss.

Only that afternoon, Molly had tried for the hundredth time to persuade Mary to give up her job and move in. But Mary had remained adamant. Furthermore, she refused to discuss Hadsea, and Molly was suffering too much pain of her own to insist as heartily as she normally did that her sister was throwing her young life away, for Molly had received a letter from Jennifer Strange.

Dear Miss Maguire, she had written. *So Lord David is to be married to Lady Cynthia after all! And after having paid court to both of us. I swear I was never more deceived. . . .*

The rest of the letter went over and over the same subject. Molly was shrewd enough to realize that the writer was motivated by spite but she also thought Jennifer had written out of rage and disappointment. So Lord David was a cad after all!

Angry tears began to form in Molly's eyes. Mary never knew how much her stronger sister clung to the dream of returning to England in triumph. Molly had worked and slaved day and night at her business with that one end in mind. Once again she would be rich and expensively dressed. She would have her Season in London and Lord David would turn and stare as she floated into the ballroom. Now her dream was spoiled by the vision of Lord David turning and staring with Lady Cynthia hanging possessively on his arm.

For the very first time she felt worn out. She climbed down from her high desk and straightened her spine and walked wearily to the shop door. She snapped up the blind and stared out into the darkness of Fulton Street. A train roared over the elevated overhead, sending small flurries of snow falling onto the street and setting the dresses swaying on their hangers.

Lady Fanny had written a kind letter, offering both girls a home in England, but both were too proud to accept charity. The only good thing out of all this mess, reflected Molly, was that Mrs. Maguire had at least returned to her normal self, putting on some much needed weight and helping busily about the shop. She stared unseeingly out of the door into the dancing snow, picturing Hadsea, wondering if Mrs. Pomfret was still at the post office and whether she had married Billy, wondering if Lord David had sold his villa. *Why, I can almost see him standing on the other side of Fulton Street,* Molly thought. *The snow must be playing tricks on my eyes.*

Another train rattled overhead, and in the flickering lights of the passing train, which cast their brief illumination down into the snowy street, she did see Lord David Manley.

"He's probably on his honeymoon," said Molly to herself, bitterly. The tall figure walked across the street and stood looking at her through the glass, his face very remote and stern. At last he said, "Aren't you going to let me in, Miss Maguire?"

She drew back the bolts and opened the door. He removed his tall silk hat and placed it on a small table and then sat down in a chair, crossing his legs and smiling at her pleasantly. "Well, this is quite like old times," said the infuriating man.

"There is a difference now, buster," said Molly. "I've gotta work for a living, see. So why don't you—"

"Make a noise like a hoop and roll away," he finished. "No I will not. I've had a damned uncomfortable journey and a damned hideous evening trying to find you."

"Why?" said Molly coldly. "Cynthia want some frocks wholesale?"

"Don't be cheeky," he said pleasantly. "I haven't seen Cynthia since that cursed ball. I really don't know why I bother with you, Molly. It's very damaging to the ego to keep laying one's heart at a girl's feet just for her to trample over."

"She rejected you," said Molly. "Well, if that doesn't beat the band!"

"Oh, don't be so dashed stupid. Trust a woman to pick up the wrong thing. If you aren't the most irritating, infuriating girl I ever came across . . ."

"Then why don't you just *leave*," screamed Molly. "Go on, vamoose, beat it, scram."

"Then I will. I damned well will just do

that very thing. You are a stupid, stubborn, thoughtless girl. Good day to you!"

The shop door slammed behind him and the little bell above the door tinkled and swayed wildly on its wire.

Gone.

Silence.

"Oh," whispered Molly to herself, "he meant he was laying his heart at *my* feet. Oh . . . !"

She flew to the shop door and crashed it open. She flew down Fulton Street under the stark black shadows cast by the King's County Elevated Railroad to where a thinner, blacker shadow was moving off into the night.

"David!" she cried, but another passing train drowned the sound of her voice.

Thank God he had stopped walking. He was standing quite still under a lamplight, staring at the snow swirling around his feet.

He turned around abruptly and started to run back when he collided full into Molly Maguire. They both slipped and fell onto the sidewalk, hanging on to each other, Molly stammering incoherent apologies and Lord David trying to kiss her mouth and shut her up. He kissed her shoulder, then her ear, then her nose, and then his mouth found its target as the elegant lord lay flat in the middle of a Fulton Street sidewalk, kissing Molly Maguire until she was breathless and then kissing her again as soon as she got her breath back.

"Whassis?" demanded the deep voice of Officer Brady, the very hairs of his gray wool uniform seeming to stand on end with shock.

"You will marry me as soon as possible," his lordship was saying.

"Oh, *yes*," sighed Miss Maguire.

Lord David took her face in his long fingers and bent his head to kiss her, oblivious of the fact that Officer Brady was prodding him in the back with his nightstick.

"Dat's Miss Maguire," exclaimed the outraged officer of the law. "Dere's no need t' take t' the streets, girl!" A taxicab came bumping over the snowy ruts, illuminating the shameless couple. Lord David got to his feet and hailed the cab and then became aware that the strong arm of the law was trying to pull him back.

Lord David stuck his hand in his pocket and withdrew several notes. "Here, Officer, drink to our health. We are to be married," he said.

"Ho, that's different," said Officer Brady, clutching the pile of notes, but the couple had already climbed into the taxicab, which had driven off. He looked down at the notes in his hand and then examined them under the streetlamp. The unmistakable features of King Edward stared up at him from the notes.

"*British* money," said Officer Brady in disgust. Then the cheering thought that he could change the filthy English money at the bank in the morning occurred to him. It further struck him that someone on his beat had once mentioned that the English pound was worth five good American dollars. Tonight, however, he would drink to Molly Maguire's health—and put it on the slate.